Vale of Hope

Grace Bourget

En Route Books and Media, LLC
Saint Louis, MO

En Route Books and Media, LLC

5705 Rhodes Avenue

St. Louis, MO 63109

Contact us at contactus@enroutebooksandmedia.com

Cover credit: Grace Bourget

© 2022 Grace Bourget

ISBN-13: 978-1-956715-74-3

Library of Congress Control Number: 2022942452

Dedicated to the Hearts of the Holy Family.

In honor of the Holy Face of Christ and Our Lady of La Salette, that it may help to dry their tears,

And in loving memory of my mother, Lisa Bourget, who brought me back to God and gave me her love of His rainbow smile.

Table of Contents

I: Rebellion 1

II: Collision.. 13

III: Lamentation... 25

IV: Illumination 45

V: Vexation 57

VI: Absolution.. 63

VII: Desperation 77

VIII: Retribution... 91

IX: Rejection.. 109

X: Inundation 123

XI: Ramification.. 129

XII: Passion... 143

XIII: Devotion... 153

XIV: Justification 165

XV: Reunion 179

XVI: Tintinnabulation 189

I

Rebellion

Disgusted, Don Carreras stood at his desk in his private study with his back to his son. It was early September, and the light in the room reflected the fire of the turning leaves outside. Sighing in frustration, he turned to look at the handsome, disheveled, reckless youth, whose lip was still bleeding.

"Paul, this is the last straw! I can't understand your continuation of this behavior! Last week you stole from Don Pedro, merely for the fun of it. I thought my punishment had driven it through your head! Now, I find that you've been thrown out of a tavern for drinking too much and starting a fight – exactly what I told you not to do!" Don Carreras shook his head angrily. "Paul, when will you ever grow up?"

His son grimaced slightly and glowered at the floor. His father sighed.

"Son. . . your mother and I love you. We have been trying to control your wildness since you were little; we are trying to help you. Do you understand that?"

Paul nodded sulkily, his wild, deep brown hair a mess.

"Son, what do you think the villagers will say of me? Their magistrate can't even control the wild behavior of his own son!" He let out his breath and then turned back to his son. "Did you go to confession last week when I told you to?"

Paul stiffened and tried to look innocent, but his father saw through the disguise and sighed.

"Oh, Paul, Paul! How is it that you don't love your religion?" His face hardened. "Think of your little sister Imelda. What will she think? Until now, I have kept your sins hidden from her. Do you think that she will still call you her Angel?"

A panicked expression crept into Paul's gray eyes. Little three-year-old Imelda loved Paul with a special love. She was delicate and often ill, and at such times the whole house fell into a state of fear and concern, afraid that it would claim her life. She needed protection, which had been provided by Paul. He had jealously guarded his job from his brothers, carrying his little sister whenever she was exhausted, caring for her when she was sick, singing her to sleep, and doing a thousand other things for her.

"Oh, Father, please don't tell her!" he cried desperately. "Please!" His father exhaled deeply.

"I have no choice. You yourself have chosen this, Paul. Your stubbornness and disobedience and dishonesty has led to this. I must tell her." He studied his son's frightened, despairing eyes.

"This is a terrible punishment for you, son, but even this cannot right your wrongs in the eyes of the townspeople. Therefore, I forbid you to see your friends, particularly that scoundrel Rodrigo, and I sentence you to aid Father Bruno in the leper colony for the next five months."

"No!" Paul cried in disgust. "Not that! Please not that!"

His father, the city's magistrate and thus one of the richer men in the town, gave him a look. "There is no getting out of this. I expect you to be gentle, obedient, and most of all, polite. There is no need to make those poor people feel any worse. I hope this punishment will make a man out of you. Otherwise, you can never hope to marry. No girl in her right mind would take you for her husband."

With that, Paul's father strode out of the room. His son trailed behind him, dreading his little sister's reaction to the news. Don Carreras knocked softly on the nursery door. In a moment, it was opened by his wife, Dona Rosita, who was holding a sweet child of three, whose golden-brown curls framed her face.

"Hello, Daddy!" she chirped, leaning out of her mother's arms to hug him.

"Hello, Princess," he answered softly, giving her a hug. "I must speak with you, my little one."

He lifted her out of his wife's arms and carried her into the nursery, leaving the door open so that Paul could stand and watch in shame. Now that his little sister was to be informed of his sins, the eighteen-year-old youth began to sweat and rubbed his hands on his tunic. His father set Imelda on the bed, pillowing her on the blankets.

"Little Blossom," he said gently, "I must talk to you about

Paul. He did something very wrong, and you must pray for him."

Imelda's brown eyes widened, and she turned them to Paul. "Angel," she said, stretching her arms out towards him. He turned away to hide the tears flooding his gray eyes and sucked his breath in to prevent a sob.

"Angel!" she repeated insistently, forcing him to come slowly to her. As soon as he was close enough, Imelda put her arms around his waist and looked up at him. "What did you do?" Her sweet brown eyes were wide and trusting.

"I just – disobeyed," he muttered, feeling his cheeks flame with shame. "What did you do?" she repeated. He hesitated, glancing at his father.

"I – I drank too much," the boy stammered. His father gave him a look, forcing him to continue. "I started a fight–"

The brown eyes faded with disappointment, but the child hugged him tightly. "You can go to the church," she said trustingly. "Please, Paul?" Her brother gazed down at her, his eyes wide. Imelda never called him by his name. Indeed, he was no longer her Angel.

Removing himself from her embrace, he stumbled out of the room, half-blinded by tears, utterly disgraced. Somehow, he made his way to the church, but once inside, he collapsed and tried to force back his tears.

Glancing up, he saw that there was no line for Confession. How he hated to go! Being judged for what his personality was inclined to do was unsufferable, except where

Imelda was concerned. He weighed further disobedience against his sister's affections and found that even his determination to avoid entering the confessional could not tip the scales in his favor. With a groan he slowly made his way inside. It was dim and cool, all sounds from outside blanketed in the velvet curtain behind him. He knew he had to say everything, no matter how it pained him; it would only torture his memory if he faked it while Imelda trusted him.

"Bless me, padre, for I have sinned," he muttered.

"Have you sinned?" the voice interrupted him from the other side of the screen.

Paul blinked. "Forsooth," he sighed.

"You know that you've sinned, then," the priest confirmed. Paul shook his head in annoyance. What was this, a grilling session?

"Verily!" the youth said, a bit more sharply than he had intended.

"I see."

Paul growled internally as the voice fell into silence. "Forgive me," he muttered again.

"Forgive you for what? You haven't confessed yet," the priest reminded him, with a soft laugh.

Splendid, now I have yet another thing I must put on my list because he's right here, Paul complained to himself. He carefully listed each sin that he knew of, realizing that Imelda would approve of none of them. He felt as though he were plucking thorn after thorn out of his skin, leaving hopelessly bloody scars. Confession concluded, he knelt awaiting his death sentence. There was silence.

"Padre?"

"I surmise," the voice came slowly, "that you don't feel a great deal of contrition for what you've just confessed, my son. Tell me of your feelings."

Feelings? In a confessional? Where was all the 'religion isn't about feelings?'

"I can hardly feel sorry for something that is in my nature," Paul grumbled. "If I want to experiment and see how easy it is to take something, I do it, and if I want to drink and break a man's nose for insulting my sister, I'll do it whether he's done something considered 'worthy' of starting a fight or not."

"You do these things because that's what you want to do?"

"Yes. . ."

"Of course, these things are in your nature. It's in human nature. Everyone wants to break someone's nose at some time. But that's not the point. The point is that we're supposed to remove these things from our nature, insofar as we can, not to embrace them. You can hardly say something you're intended to remove is a part of your personality. No, defending your sister is your personality; rebelliousness, pride, intemperance, and anger are your faults. And faults are like a crack in the earth; they must be mended as much as they can be and worked around and avoided as you are able to, and in time they will heal like the scars you feel from your fight."

Paul had no answer to this; now he was only feeling the pain of Imelda's rejection and the pain of kneeling here in disgrace.

"I don't feel sorry," he said, "except that I know my sister won't love me as much until I tell her I've been to confession."

"Your sins can't be forgiven unless you at least try to be contrite for the right reasons," the priest murmured. "Even if you don't feel it, if you will to be sorry, and desire to be truly sorry for offending the God who made you and died for you, and suffers for you every day at every trial and tribulation you face, and with every sin you commit, then you can be forgiven. Do you have any reason not to love Him? You can tell me without fear."

"I suppose He has been good to me. . . I just. . . don't feel close to Him, and I just want to do what I want to do."

"But He doesn't want you to do that. He did His Father's Will and gave up everything He had, to be with you. Don't you want to be with Him for His sake? You know your heart will feel lighter if you do."

Paul had to admit that the padre was making sense, and there was nothing he could say. He supposed he really did owe God a good confession, but the hard part was knowing he'd have to try not to do all the things that came to his wild heart, and the thought that his family would be glad that they had convinced him – Paul knew he had to ignore his pride and try not to think of any of the consequences, or he'd never make it. He asked for absolution; this time it was given without hesitation, but with a sizeable penance.

Knowing that he must not return home without doing his penance lest his Imelda still be upset, Paul knelt in a pew and began praying. He had never had much faith in prayer, but this time he found himself begging God to not let Imelda be upset with him any longer. He wanted to be her Angel again. He was going to have to try not to lose her affections. He didn't realize that his resolution was made depending on his own strength and not his Savior's, spelling failure.

But for now, his heart was lightened. He wasn't sure how his family would react when he returned. Paul paced in the church gardens and finally found the courage to walk back down the dirt road to his family's villa.

"Angel!" Paul spun around to see his mother and Imelda seated in a sunlit, rose-filled grotto, where Our Lady's image was crowned every May. Imelda leapt to her feet and ran to him.

I'm still her Angel! Paul thought with delight. His face lit up and he caught her up, swinging her around as they both laughed gleefully. "Do you want to dance, my little Imelda?" he cried jubilantly.

His sister giggled, and setting her down on a graceful marble bench, Paul began to waltz with her, humming her favorite tune. At the last note, he scooped her off and spun her around again before carrying her over to his mother, with a pleading expression in his eyes.

Dona Rosita, from whom Imelda had inherited her sweet

gracefulness, looked like a rose herself in her lovely gown and soft white mantle. She hugged him fondly. Paul bent close to her so that his face was near to hers, and he glanced into her gray eyes, smiling softly.

"Are you still upset, Mother dear?" She smiled and kissed his cheek.

"After one confesses one's sins, they are forgotten by God, and so I try to forget them, too." Paul kissed her forehead.

"It's rather warm out here," he observed, glancing up at the summer sun. He looked down at Imelda, who was still in his arms. "Are you thirsty, my precious?" She nodded, nestling her cheek against his heart.

"Mommy made some lemonade," she suggested. Smiling, he placed her in their mother's arms. Because the grotto was full of shade and was therefore cool, he did not worry about her becoming overheated.

It would be rather pleasant to sit here in front of Our Lady, he thought, glancing at the pink, yellow, and white blossoms.

"I'll bring it out here," he offered. Both happily agreed, and Paul jogged into the villa and poured lemonade for the three of them. When he returned, he handed each a cup and seated himself on the ground, leaning against his mother's knee. Imelda's face was almost hidden by the glass as she drank. She was so adorable that Paul smiled to himself and plucked a pink rose, which he slipped into her curls.

"I love you, little Blossom," he said affectionately.

"Love Angel," she replied, removing the cup and glancing around for something to wipe lemonade from her cheeks. Gently, her brother dried her lips with the edge of his sleeve.

"I should have gotten you a smaller cup," he teased. She giggled.

"If I had another cup, I would not have so much lemonade!"

He grinned at her. "You sound like me!"

Giggling, she reached out with one slightly sticky little hand and swiped at his hair. "Paul is a goose," she declared to her mother. Dona Rosita laughed.

"He certainly is!" She laid her hand on his shoulder.

Don Carreras exited the house and saw them seated in the grotto. Paul tensed and arose, prepared for another lecture. His father, however, did not appear to be upset. He approached them, smiling.

"Did you go to confession, Paul?" His son nodded and Don Carreras clapped him on the back. "Good lad!" he said approvingly and tugged one of Imelda's curls.

"Daddy, did you know that Paul is a goose?" she asked, intent on learning whether angels could also be feathered birds. Her father inspected Paul gravely.

"I think I see some feathers," he admitted, and laughing, he tackled his son. They wrestled playfully for a few moments, much to his mother and sister's amusement.

Finally, Paul's father released him, and they scrambled to their feet, with bits of grass clinging to their tunics and in their hair. Imelda leaned over and plucked one out of Paul's slightly curly, thick brown hair.

"Green feathers?"

"No, I'm a grass beast now," he chuckled and made a face at her. The child laughed, but the sound trailed away as one little hand went to her heart. Father, mother, and brother all reached for her at once.

"Sweetheart. . .?" Don Carreras took his daughter's arms and looked into her face. "Does it hurt?"

For a moment Paul felt as though it had begun to rain. The sun shone again a moment later when Imelda gave a bright smile. "I'm alright now, Daddy."

"Hm, we're going to have to get my little girl some medicine all the way from the moon, aren't we," he asked, scooping her up and bouncing her in his arms.

"How you going to the moon," she demanded, "when the sun made it go away again?"

"Don't worry, your daddy knows how to get there," he promised and gave her a kiss. "Time to take you inside."

Once Imelda was playing happily with her older sister, Marina, Don Carreras took Paul aside, saying, "I am going to go and see the Padre. I want to find out when he will start taking you. Please, Paul, try and be charitable with the lepers and please don't be upset. You brought this upon yourself. If you learn obedience, there will be no more punishments like this."

He hugged his son affectionately, seemingly aware of the

cold knot that was forming in his son's stomach. "Five months will pass quickly, you will see," he said comfortingly. "It will help you more than you know, and that will help Imelda."

Paul summoned a faint smile and went and wandered the gardens, nervously pretending that all was well as Imelda waved from her window and the twins pelted him with rose-buds.

When his father returned, he informed Paul that he and Padre Bruno would start tomorrow at dawn, when it was still cool. The leper colony was some six miles outside of the town, in a little-visited area in a dry piece of land, nearly devoid of grass. Dreading the following day, Paul spent the rest of the day making sure Imelda was kept quiet for the sake of her little heart.

II

Collision

The next morning, wagon wheels were heard rolling up the drive, crunching on the gravel. Paul sat up in bed, his hair disheveled, and rubbed his eyes. Why was someone coming to visit this early in the morning? He glanced outside, for his window faced the drive, and saw a plain wagon, loaded with barrels of food and supplies, stop outside. Fr. Bruno alighted and spoke with whomever had opened the door.

At that moment, the bedroom door flew open and Paul's sixteen-year-old sister Marina, the family's little healer, ran into the room in a breathless flurry. "Haste, Paul! Father Bruno is here to take you to the leper colony!" She dashed out, and Paul leapt out of bed, his heart pounding, and tripped on the bedclothes.

"Fie upon me!" he moaned, hastily pulling open drawers and closets, attempting to gather his clothes in twenty seconds. "I would have to sleep late!"

Darting into the next room, he hastily changed, splashed icy water on his face, and ran downstairs, running his fingers through his hair and drying his face on his sleeve. He nearly crashed into a wall, dashed down the second flight of steps, collided with his younger brother Josef, jumped aside, leapt down the last three stairs, stumbled, and skidded to a stop in front of his father, who had been watching him in amusement.

"Hail the dawn, Paul," he greeted his son, who flung his hair out of his eyes. "You have a wonderful task ahead of you. I expect you to be kind and to give the Padre whatever assistance he requires. You will follow every word he speaks, for this is one part of your penance. Treat the ill as though they were the same as you. You ought to be home by six; have a good day, obey Father Bruno, and be good."

He stepped aside and Paul reluctantly started for the wagon but had only gotten as far as the open doorway when a cry of "Angel! Angel!" halted him. He turned in time to see Imelda bouncing downstairs in her trailing nightgown, with her mother following. Reaching the last step, Imelda ran to him, and he crouched and scooped her up, holding her close.

"Why do you have to leave me, Angel?" she mumbled into his shoulder. "You supposed to take me through the garden today and play horsey with me."

"I know, poppet, but. . . I've been a bad angel, so I must go. You'll have to play with Momma and Marina, and I'll play with you another time," he promised.

"But you always play with me, Angel!" Imelda looked like she was about to cry. "I thought you were a good angel now 'cause you went to church."

Paul was aware that the rest of his family was watching with interest, but he also had the nagging feeling he needed to get outside to the Padre.

"Ah, no, being a good angel takes practice," he whispered, "but I promise I'll bring you a present, so will you give a rainbow smile? Come on, where is it?" He gently tickled her cheek until that sunny smile came out and Imelda shook her golden curls and giggled.

"Now be a good girl while I'm gone, Imelda," he told her. "Don't let yourself become overheated or too cold or upset or lonely without me or–"

"Paul," his father said gently. "She knows."

Slightly embarrassed, Paul reluctantly let go of his only excuse to stay home.

"God be with ye, my son," Don Carreras smiled, and squeezed his son's shoulder. Paul then met Father Bruno at the wagon. The priest didn't seem surprised or disgruntled at the long wait.

"God's morning! All ready?"

"Certe, Padre," Paul muttered and clambered into the cart, trying to quell the queasy feeling in his stomach as he thought of what lay ahead.

"That is well; vamanos!" Father Bruno said cheerfully. He sat down beside him, took the reins, clucked to the hard-working bays, and they were on their way.

Paul's heartbeat faltered as the cart rolled out into the countryside. He was frightened, he owned, for the disease of leprosy could enter his veins and make him as much an outcast as – well, as he already felt he was. Only the thought of little Imelda gave him courage. Father Bruno sensed the youth's problem and gave him a smile as the villa disappeared behind them.

"Don't worry, my son," he said reassuringly. "God will give you the courage if you ask Him and trust that He will give it to you."

"Why should He, He's punishing me isn't He?" Paul retorted.

"Purifying you is more like it," the priest replied. "The more you accept it with trust, love, and humility, the less He'll need to watch you suffer. An odd way of putting it, to your ears, I'm sure; but it hurts Him to see you suffer the way it hurts you to suffer. The Madonna in Valencia – the Lady of the Forsaken – surely would be a good mother to you, Paul."

Paul shook his head in confusion but dutifully muttered a Pater and an Ave under his breath. Gradually, the road became rough, and the priest turned the horse onto a little-traveled dirt track. Wild, rocky terrain surrounded them as far as the eye could see. A quiet breeze fluttered the white and pink petals of the autumn snowflake growing scattered among the stones.

Paul shivered involuntarily. There was a beauty in this wilderness that he couldn't see; even the sunshine seemed cold with his fear. It wasn't long before the wagon came to a rocky promontory, overlooking a small valley, and rolled to a stop.

Paul sucked in his breath and went very still. So, this was

the sight he had dreaded. Roughly carven caves served as dim, cold homes for the sick; a fire burned in the middle of the clearing below, over which simmered of pot of liquid, a poor kind of soup, Paul supposed. A small creek ran through the vale, adding some peace and beauty, as did little clumps of tall grasses and bobbing snowflake blossoms.

Men and women moved through the camp, attending to their chores or stretching their afflicted limbs. Cloaks, tunics, and cowls in muted colors hid their blemished skin. A young woman stooped over the pot and stirred it; an old man shuffled across the courtyard and sat down in the shade of one of the caves to speak with a younger one.

A group of women stood near to the valley wall of the promontory, to the left and below of the wagon. They spoke of their families and the rosary in hushed voices while they did their wash.

Several children were giggling and playing a game, splashing in the brook while their mothers looked on, smiling. Soft laughter came from one corner of the court-yard, where a few young men were gathered around their mothers. A family knelt in the dust of their cave, praying.

"Welcome to the Vale of Hope," Padre Bruno said solemnly. He glanced at the youth. "Surprised?"

Paul nodded dumbly, and Father Bruno clucked to the horse, nudging it down a sloping incline to the left, which curved downwards over the caves and into the courtyard. Instantly, the young men got to their feet, the praying family paused and came out, and the children came running to the wagon, shrieking.

"Hello, my little ones!" Father Bruno cried, and laughing, dismounted and scooped them up.

"Padre, come play with us!" the children cried.

Chuckling, the priest allowed himself to be wrangled into a game of tug-of-war, leaving Paul staring. He swallowed hard when he realized that the gathering adults must be wondering at his presence. The youth hastily dismounted on the other side of the cart, pretending to busy himself loosening a strap. He leaned his forehead against the high sides of the cart. Every muscle in his body was shaking.

"I want to go home!" he whispered, his voice trembling with hot tears. "Why do you want me to be afraid?" he asked with a sudden growl. "I can be better without this!"

Truly . . .? a voice seemed to say inside of him. Paul shook his head, knowing he was grasping at straws. With trembling fingers, he blinked back his tears and began untying the strap. The Padre's voice broke in.

"Oh, Paul, Paul!"

Quickly mastering himself, Paul poked his head around the side of the cart.

"Yes, Padre?"

"Would you untie the straps and bring me the big box, please?"

"Certainly." Paul's outward calmness belied the humiliation in his heart as he untied the straps and clambered into the cart. Being the rebellious son of wealthy parents, he had always decided that he was above any type of labor. Yes, he was a shirker. But he had promised to obey whatever the Padre said, no matter how much pain rent through his proud being.

Finding the oversized crate, Paul had a flicker of hope. Would the Padre let him merely unload the cart and leave the rest to him? Surely, that was a far better arrangement for both.

After all, what do I know about such things? Paul thought. The youth lifted the heavy box easily and jumped out of the wagon. Father Bruno turned and smiled.

"Good! Bring it and set it right here, Paul, please." The youth obeyed, though his steps faltered as he drew nearer to the lepers.

"Alright, come and see what friends have donated for you, my poppets!" the priest said, bending and prying the box open.

"Ooh!" the children cried, crowding around and peering inside. Colorful toys half-filled the box; on the very top were garments to replace those that were too worn already.

"Paul, help me hand these out, please," the priest said. The boy felt as though he had been stabbed. There was nothing he could do but force a smile and try to hand out the play-things as though it was an everyday occurrence with ordinary people. He couldn't stop thinking about what would happen if he contracted the disease from them and had to live there with them. Hardly hearing the happy cries of the children as they ran off, Paul turned to his companion to see what torture he was in for next.

"Come, Paul; we must finish unloading." Father Bruno beckoned the youth to follow him and they returned to the wagon.

"Padre, what are those children doing here?" Paul whispered, taking a barrel from him.

"They contracted leprosy," the priest answered soberly, "and rather than being separated from their sick little ones, the parents came, too, and help around here. Of course, many of them become sick. Some, however, haven't, such as Henry and Marietta." The priest pointed both adults out to him. Paul sighed.

"Why does God let that happen? Why? And my baby sister, with her heart–!" He started to slam down a box to release his anger, but the priest stopped him, gently touching his hand.

"Not such a good idea – eggs," he said with a small smile.

"Oh." Paul set it down carefully.

"God lets things like this happen to perfect us," the priest continued.

"But they are innocent children!" Paul protested.

The priest nodded thoughtfully. "We aren't always meant to know why, until we're standing with Him and can see the river of our lives running together in a beautiful pattern we can never see on Earth. One reason may be that He doesn't do it to punish them, Paul. Rather, to glorify them and us; seeing their suffering may help us to offer up our own; seeing how they bear it with smiles, love, and joy, despite pain, teaches us how to accept everything from God with a smile and gratitude. Haven't you noticed how Imelda lets go of her suffering because she wants to bring her sweetness to your family, without the bitterness she could otherwise feel? She's just a child, Paul. You're almost a grown man. Isn't she an example for you?"

The youth frowned slightly and said nothing, continuing to unload the wagon. With the task finished, he found himself drenched in sweat and requested leave to take a break.

"Go ahead: I don't want you to get heat stroke on your first day! Oh, and the water in the brook is clean; don't worry about that." And shouldering a barrel, Father Bruno headed off to deliver it to one of the families. Paul sighed and glanced around.

To his relief, none of the lepers were nearby, having all withdrawn to the shade of the caves. Kneeling, Paul splashed some water on his face. It felt very good after being so over-heated and dehydrated. He washed off the dust accumulated from the long ride and rolled up his sleeves, immersing his arms in the water and then drinking long and deep. The water was cold and sweet. He sat back with a sigh and glanced up at the sun.

It was almost midday, and he was becoming hungry. He

grew restless and impatient waiting for the Padre to return and give him another task. Another half-hour passed before Paul finally glimpsed the priest approaching, deep in thought. The boy scrambled to his feet and met him.

Before he could speak, Father Bruno's words tolled what seemed to be a death knell. "Paul, I have another task for you. I was told of a girl who arrived yesterday. She is very young, about your age, and is very sad. Her name is Iria Ramirez. She left her family as soon as she found out she had contracted the disease and won't permit them to visit her. In fact, she hasn't told them where she is, for fear they will become as ill as she. Iria's a self-sacrificing girl and tries to focus on everyone's pain but her own, yet I think her heart needs healing. I want you to go and talk with her, Paul," the priest said quietly. "I feel the two of you can help each other."

"But–" Paul began desperately.

"Paul!" Father Bruno said softly but firmly. "I want you to do this for me, chico."

At that moment, a girl garbed in blue exited one of the caves and made her way to the creek, a pail in one hand, drawing her veil closer to her face with the other.

"There she is," Father Bruno said softly. "Now go, Paul." He then went to attend his own work.

Paul swallowed hard. Handing out toys was one thing – speaking to this girl in close proximity was quite another! What would he even say? How could he even manage to be polite as his father had instructed? He wanted to cover his face with his handkerchief, but he didn't dare. At least, he could stand upwind, he hoped.

He moaned softly. Gathering his courage, he walked towards the girl, who was kneeling beside a few tumbled large rocks at the creek bank. The girl cupped her hands and drank, then slowly dipped her pail in the water, admiring the sparkle of the sun. Paul paused a few yards away and hesitated before advancing.

"Buenos dias."

The girl glanced up sharply, drawing her veil closer to her face. He could only see her soft eyes. "Good morning." Her voice was soft and hesitant.

Paul bit his tongue and fumbled for the only thing he could think of to say. "Is your name Iria?"

The girl nodded, lifting her pail out of the water and setting it beside her. Paul paused, unsure of what to say next.

"The Padre wished me to speak with you."

"He is a good man. So are you," she added, glancing up at him, her face hidden by the shadow from her veil, "for helping us."

Paul flushed, ashamed, and it did not help that the sun was beating down on his dark hair and making him hotter. "Verily, I didn't wish to come," he heard himself saying, forced to tell the truth because of the girl's voice, full of trust and gratitude. "My father punished me by having me help the Padre."

The girl thought a moment, slowly turning her head and

studying the sparkling water. "Still," she said, "you came."

"I had to."

"Another boy might have run away and shirked his duty."

"The thought would have occurred to me if the situation had been more forgiving." Paul's voice was so bitter that the girl hastily arose as if to go.

"Where are you going?" the youth exclaimed.

"I must go – I have work to do," she answered, still moving away.

"Wait!"

Iria paused but did not look at him. "You don't have to speak with me if you don't want to," she said softly. "I know how you feel. I understand."

"Iria -" Paul broke off, more uncertain than before. "Padre told me to–"

"You already did. You did as he bid you, and that is very well!" the girl answered gently. "I appreciate his thoughtfulness." She vanished into one of the caves.

Paul stood there, ashamed of his own conduct and berating himself for it. Surely, the Padre would be disappointed if he knew. The youth sighed. He went back to the wagon and sat down with his back against it, folded his arms on his knees, and dropped his head.

III

Lamentation

That night, Paul dismounted from the wagon, fatigued, emotionally exhausted, and wanting to take a bath more than anything else. He muttered a goodnight to Father Bruno, wearily turned the doorknob, and dragged himself up the stairs.

Once in his room, he scrubbed his hands vigorously with soap, rinsed them, and tugged wearily on the bell pull. He drowsily asked the servant to bring bathwater. He then locked the door and took three baths in succession before he was satisfied that he couldn't possibly have a germ left on him.

He dressed and collapsed briefly on the bed before mustering the strength to make his way downstairs, where he knew his family was taking dinner. They were awaiting him at the table when he entered.

"Angel!" Imelda shrieked and leaned out of her chair to reach him.

"Evening, Paul!" his parents greeted him with a smile.

Paul muttered a hello and tousled Imelda's curls as he sank down into his chair. He regarded the table spread with food as though it were something new to him.

Crusty bread, blackberries and grapes, and chestnuts formed the centerpiece, while a casserole of beef, orange juice, bacon, and saffron was the main part of the meal. The youth's gray eyes brightened when he saw his favorite dish, chopped spinach cooked in goat's milk with cheese and bacon.

"Would you like me to serve you some, Paul?" his elder brother, Diego, offered.

"You'd better; if you hand me that tray, I'll eat everything on it."

Diego grinned and served him while Marina poured some wine for her brother. The savory spinach and sweet wine improved Paul's mood considerably. That is, until his father asked the obvious question.

"How was your first day, Paul?"

Paul kicked back his chair and debated whether the bad news was a good idea. His family clearly wanted an honest answer whether it was negative or not, so he gave in. "In faith – it was a disaster. I accidentally ruined a maiden's day, the heat was detrimental to my mood, I was stung by a bee, and then wrenched my hand retrieving one of the children's toys that was stuck in the side of the rock wall."

Marina and the young twins, Juan and Josef, stopped eating and stared at him.

"Children?" Marina gasped. "There are children at the camp?"

Paul nodded. "Five of them. Three boys and two girls."

Imelda was looking from one sibling to another, still holding her spoonful of soup in midair. "If they're sick, why don't I go there since I'm sick?" she wanted to know.

Don Carreras gave his children a warning look and gently explained to Imelda that it was a far different type of sickness.

"Don't worry, my sweeting, you don't need to go there," he promised.

"But why do they have to go there?" she inquired.

"Because they don't want anyone else to get sick from them, poppet."

"Oh! Won't you get sick from me?" Imelda asked in sudden terror. Her father cuddled her.

"No, no, no one's able to get sick from you, precious girl!"

Reassured, Imelda tugged at her father's cross that hung around his neck. "But it's very sad; Daddy, can Paul give them my toys?"

"They have enough toys, Imelda dear," Paul said quickly. "They aren't sad, really, but if you want to do something for them – um, well you could say your prayers for them."

"That's a perfect idea," Dona Rosita said, taking her daughter in her arms. "Speaking of prayers, it's your bedtime, darling. Give everyone a kiss, and we'll go put you to bed and give you your medicine, all the way from the moon!"

Imelda dutifully gave a kiss to her father and siblings and waved as her mother carried her up the stairs.

Paul's aching muscles then threw him onto the nearest couch. "Five whole months of taking three baths a day," he muttered. He dropped his arm down over his eyes and groaned.

"You took three baths today?" Josef asked incredulously.

"Sometimes, I think he takes a bath once a week," Juan smirked.

"That would be three months minus a day," Diego corrected Paul, ignoring his little brother's joke.

"I don't think three baths is a good idea for your skin," his father observed. "At least limit it to two."

Paul groaned again and dropped his arm, looking over at his father. "I wouldn't feel safe doing that, especially with Imelda. If I catch it, she'll be the first to take it from me."

"Sometimes, I think you worry too much, son. Cautiousness is good; scrupulosity is not. It only damages you more in the long run."

Paul just shook his head in disbelief. How could that be more dangerous than being careful not to catch leprosy? His brain was too tired to try and understand. He sat up gingerly, wincing as his aching muscles rebelled.

"I guess I'll go to bed – see you in the morning. Oh!" He groaned and fell back as he remembered that he was going to have to do it all over again the next day.

"It will get easier, Paul," his father comforted him. Paul groaned again and pulled himself to his feet.

"Goodnight," he mumbled wearily, and himself back up the stairs and into his room, where he collapsed in bed and instantly fell asleep.

The next morning, Paul again slept late and had to rush out the door. The day was cooler, and Paul hoped that everything would go more smoothly the second time. When the pair reached the camp, the children again ran to see Father Bruno and begged him to tell them the story of Jesus multiplying the loaves and the fishes. This left Paul on his own for a time.

He kicked small stones about aimlessly, but his thoughts couldn't turn from his guilt over Iria. His father had told him he needed to apologize. If Father Bruno had instructed him to speak charitably with Iria, then it was necessary to befriend her.

He watched the lepers as they accomplished their daily chores. Some he could hardly tell were afflicted. Others had scars or strange marks on their faces and fingers. Some had trouble feeling pain due to nerve damage and had to have a constant companion in case they became injured and didn't realize it. However, none seemed to exhibit the worst symptoms of leprosy.

Paul straightened, feeling slightly better. The second of his worst fears seemed unfounded; there were no missing fingers or open wounds, at least that he could see. What he could not see was Iria.

He felt awful, for hadn't his father told him to be kind to these sufferers and that there was no need to make them feel any worse than they surely did? The youth had promptly failed and felt ashamed for disappointing his father. What use was his confession and all his resolutions to curb his wildness for the sake of Imelda's gentle heart? Thoughts of taverns and strong wine mingled with a growing self-bitterness. Thankfully, it was interrupted by Father Bruno.

"I'll be celebrating Mass now," he said. "I'll need you to be my altar-server, son."

If that wasn't the craziest thing Paul had ever heard! A rebellious wine-drinking altar-server formed an incongruous picture in his mind. He had no choice but to say yes, although he was sure to ruin the Mass with his lack of instruction. Once again, the Padre seemed to read his mind.

"Don't worry; I'll tell you what to do," came the assurance. Somehow, Paul managed to carry out his duties as well as could be expected.

After pouring water and wine into the chalice for the offering, he noticed Iria on the outskirts of the gathered lepers. Her head was dropped slightly, and her veil hid her eyes, but she seemed clearly distraught about something. But every time anyone turned her way, she straightened and gave them a soft smile that belied any pain. Paul nearly forgot his next task until Father Bruno caught his attention. The boy quickly put Iria out of his mind and carefully carried out his duties until the Mass was over.

He aided Father Bruno to put away the supplies for Mass, but the youth was still distracted. Were his actions yesterday the cause of her distress? he wondered. The need to apologize despite his rebellious feelings kept nagging at his mind until he could think of little else. Maybe he was the last person in the world she wanted to see, he decided. Apologizing could make it worse. Surely, anyone would understand such a reason for not doing as he had been instructed.

The Padre glanced at him keenly. "Paul, something is troubling you, my son. What is it?" The priest seated himself and watched the boy, who started at his voice.

Paul struggled with the urge to deny that something was wrong and to hide his mistake, at least from the priest. Was that any worse than admitting it to his own father? He moaned and sat down on the ground. Paul cast a pebble into the creek. For a moment, there was silence.

"I . . . upset Iria yesterday."

Father Bruno said nothing, but watched him quietly.

"I didn't mean to – I just don't want to be here!" he exclaimed in frustration. "Of all the things I could be doing, this isn't it, and what if I bring home leprosy and Imelda or anyone else in my family gets it?! Oh," he groaned. "I can tell that Iria is still upset, and I can't get the need to apologize out of my mind, but I'm sure to only make things worse, and what if I catch leprosy from her then? Oh, a plague upon me!" The boy got to his feet and paced for a moment. "My father told me not to upset them, and I failed the first chance I had."

"Paul. . . I guarantee you that you won't be catching leprosy." Father Bruno gazed at him, awaiting the inevitable disbelief.

"You can't know that," Paul said sharply.

"Yes, I do know that. Look, Paul, apologize," Father Bruno said calmly. "The fact that the need to apologize is growing in your mind means that it's what you need to do. It may make her feel better. But whatever happens, don't worry about leprosy."

Paul sighed, looked at the ground, and walked away to find Iria. He found the girl standing in the shade of a cave, speaking softly to an old woman while a few children played nearby. Paul frowned and hovered just outside of the blinding sunshine, waiting for her and rehearsing his apology a dozen different ways.

It was a full five minutes before the girl came towards him with some trepidation. The youth was so intent on his thoughts that he started at her footsteps.

"Iria!" She had almost passed him, but stopped, turning her face half towards him.

"Yes?"

"Iria – I wanted to apologize for how I acted yesterday. I didn't intend to insult you, it's just that. . . I was afraid."

"I know," the girl said simply. "I understand your fear. You don't have to speak to me; it's my wish just as strongly as yours that you don't receive our illness."

"Father Bruno wishes me to," Paul said anxiously. "I promised my father I would do anything he says. And you – I mean, I thought you were upset this morning when I saw you."

Iria shook her head. "It wasn't because of you," she told

him gently. She took a deep breath and seemed to hold back a sob. "I must go now."

"But why? I'm supposed to talk to you," Paul retorted. If he didn't fulfill his mission, he worried that he would be given a worse task.

"If you need me to say that I forgive you, I forgive you!" Iria cried, breaking down, and turned in haste to leave.

"Iria!" His hand flew out involuntarily and he barely stopped himself from grabbing her arm. "What have I done now?"

"Done? You haven't done anything! Please, I must go," she entreated him.

"If I haven't offended you, why are you distraught?" he demanded. The girl's lips trembled. Paul blew out his breath in frustration. "I may not be an angel and you might be dead to society, but that doesn't mean we can't have a decent conversation!"

"Oh, let me go, please!" she begged, turning and trying to flee.

"Iria!" he exclaimed, gently catching her sleeve. But at that moment, someone called to the girl, and she slipped from his grasp with an unintelligible goodbye. Paul stared after her, disgusted and disgruntled. He had failed yet again.

"Why do I have to be so rough?" he muttered angrily to himself. He felt twice as badly as before, and twice as perplexed as how to solve the problem. Apparently, another apology would do no good, as he had only upset Iria further.

He scowled and kicked a stone against the rock wall behind him before striding off to rejoin Father Bruno, dreading revealing his failure and half-consciously trying to think up an excuse.

~

The next few days passed much the same: Paul served at Mass, helped with supplies and repairs, aided the children when they lost one of their toys, read stories from the Bible to them when Father Bruno asked him to, and became even more frustrated about Iria. He hardly saw her and began to feel that she was avoiding him. After a week had passed, he realized that she was avoiding everybody.

Why was his concern growing? he wondered. He had hardly even spoken to her, so there was no real reason for it. The boy tried to dismiss the feeling. Failing, he tried to laugh it off and chalk it up to guilt. Then he blamed himself for Iria's curious disappearance and was in such high dudgeon that every inconvenience, be it as simple as being unable to find his breakfast, made him fume.

After a second week of this, he gave up in exasperation and headed off, determined to corner Iria and find out what was wrong. It would appear the Padre's comment on such strong feelings were correct.

Paul first inquired of Father Bruno whether he had seen her, and when he received an answer in the negative, began to inquire among the children, who were Iria's favorites.

One child piped up that he had seen her fetching water an hour ago, but that was the best answer he could get. With a distracted thank you, Paul walked away to find someone else to ask. He was halfway to the cave nearest the wagon when he heard Father Bruno hailing him.

"Paul, Paul!"

The youth turned and jogged back. "Yes?"

"Iria just had me hear her confession. You can find her in the second cave on your left. That is, if you want to go in."

The last words were a casual but obvious challenge. Paul swallowed hard, braced himself, and entered the cave.

He proceeded cautiously, trying to breathe lightly. He passed several hewed-out rooms, in which some of the lepers lay on straw mattresses. Paul peered anxiously into each one but continued on when he did not see Iria. He began to wonder if he had entered the wrong cave and considered backtracking, thinking that he was nearing the end. He was surprised when it burrowed deeper into the rock.

He saw another room and glanced in. A woman was lying on a bed carved out of the wall. A nun, one of a group who came frequently to tend to the sick, was bending over her giving her – medicine? Then Paul realized, to his fright, that this was a makeshift hospital for the lepers.

If Iria is in here, what in the world is she doing? the boy wondered fearfully, and hastened onwards. Slowly, he saw the rock-hewed rooms disappear, and he began thinking that he had taken a wrong turn, if not the wrong cave. At that moment, he stumbled abruptly to a halt. The corridor had widened into a wide, circular room with a skylight cut into the ceiling. It was empty, except for–

"Iria!" Paul gasped. She was crouching beside a young man, who lay on a straw-mattress on a low rock ledge. The soft sounds of her sobs and whispered words finally met Paul's ears, and he stood there, frightened. He did not want to interrupt, but he couldn't turn away. Soft footsteps sounded behind him and then a hand settled on his shoulder.

"It's Henry . . . he's dying of cancer. He accompanied Iria here when she found that she was stricken with leprosy, despite her protests, and has stayed with her as her guardian. He is her first and closest cousin. They are intensely loyal and fond of each other," Father Bruno murmured. "I am to give him Last Rights."

Paul gulped, unsettled by the nearness of the man's death and unable to bear the girl's grief. Her words reached their ears, weighted with such sorrow that it was hard for even Father Bruno to listen.

"Oh, Henry, please linger with me!" the girl begged him, unable to raise her tear-filled voice above a whisper. "I still need you! You are all I have left– " she broke off as a sob choked her. "Mother and Father and my siblings cannot come – ever–" Henry weakly raised his hand and gently touched her hair.

"Ssh," he coughed, "little sister, don't cry. . . ." His voice was very hoarse and weak. He didn't have much time left. "You know you won't have to worry about me, my sweeting." He coughed again, and Iria quickly hushed him.

"Hush," she whispered anxiously, tucking the blankets more comfortably around him. "You shouldn't be talking, Henry."

"It doesn't matter now." He shook his head. "There's no time, Iria. You don't need me as your guardian now. There are people here who love you, and the Padre has promised to be as a father to you as long as he may. You're strong, Iria! I've done all that I can for you on this earth, and now I'll be praying for you in Heaven, God willing, if He take my soul!" His voice faded for a moment. "I can do more good there than on earth, little 'Ria."

"I know," Iria whispered tearfully. "I know, but it's not knowing. . .and . . . being alone. I want you so badly!"

"You have the little ones," Henry reminded her weakly. "They love you, little sister."

"I know, and I love them, too! I am so afraid though; I need an anchor so badly, but without you–"

"You have our Mother. She will never abandon you, nor will her Son." Henry coughed and Iria gently soothed him, smoothing his brow and murmuring tenderly to him while she wept.

"Iria, be strong!" whispered Henry urgently. "I've watched you grow even in your suffering, and I know that you have everything in you that you need, if you keep God with you. Think, think, little girl – I will be in Heaven in a few minutes – with God my Savior and Our Queen and the saints and angels. It will be beautiful, Iria! And I will have roses and irises for you and graces from Our Queen. I will pray for them for you, and you will get them! Iria, you will get them, I promise! Holy girl! Saintly girl! Wonderful girl!"

He was weeping openly at his cousin's fear and grief, but was smiling, too, to give her courage, and a tearful smile blossomed on the girl's face.

"I love you!" Iria laid her head on his shoulder, weeping.

"Don't cry, 'Ria," Henry pleaded, gently patting her back. "Not for me. Promise me you won't."

"I promise," Iria whispered, forcing herself to be quiet. "Will you be alright?"

"Always," Henry murmured. "I'll send you God's smile, and you'll know that everything, everything! Is well. Now where's the smile I love. . .?" Iria forced a smile for him and gave him a kiss. Henry turned his eyes to the doorway.

"Padre, I'm ready."

Father Bruno nodded, and the ceremony quietly proceeded. Then he lifted a crucifix for Henry to see.

"Will you kiss Him, Henry?"

"Yes!" he gasped, and Father Bruno gently laid the crucifix on Henry's lips. He kissed it eagerly, kissing the Lord's hands, feet, side, and bleeding brow.

"May God keep you, my son," Father Bruno said softly, watching as Henry's breathing quickened. He was nearly gone, and Iria grasped his hand tightly in both of her little ones, tears running down her cheeks. She grew still and quiet. Iria caressed her cousin's cheek and gave him the smile he had asked for.

"I love you, Henry!" she whispered, realizing it was the last time she would say it to him before he left the land of the living.

"I love you, too!" he whispered. "Be strong! We will always love you! Jesus, Mary, Joseph!" His features began to relax . . . slowly his hand slipped from Iria's.

"Henry . . ." She gazed down at him and closed her eyes. "I promise, I promise," she whispered, choking, and gently laid his hand back on his heart.

Paul, on his knees, realized that tears were running down his face. He discretely dried them on his sleeve as the priest drew the blankets over Henry's lifeless body. He shepherded the girl outside into the startling sunlight. Paul followed.

"My son, tell some of the men to remove his body and prepare it for the funeral," Father Bruno whispered, and guided Iria into one of the other caves, where he handed her over to Marietta and the children.

~

That night, Paul dismounted from the wagon in silence, quietly entered the side door of the house and went to the back stairs. Diego happened to be coming down and smiled when he saw him.

"Good evening, Paul! How did you fare today?" Paul didn't seem to hear him as he brushed past. "Paul? Paul, is something wrong?" His younger brother shut the door to his room without answering, and Diego stared after him with a troubled frown.

When Paul appeared in the dining room, he had trouble replying to his family's delighted greetings, and when Imelda gave him her rainbow smile and asked for a kiss it didn't seem to register. He looked at her as though his mind were a million miles away. It was indeed miles away, though only as far as the leper camp.

Dona Rosita and Don Carreras looked at each other as Paul's siblings all contemplated him mutely.

"Paul?" Marina ventured. "Are you feeling well? Did something happen?" She stretched out her hand to touch his shoulder and he jumped.

"Paul, what is it?" his father asked gently.

Silence. Marina and her mother shared an anxious look. Imelda was staring at him with apprehension and confusion, leaving her bread to disintegrate in the stew in which she had been dunking it. Even Juan and Josef looked at each other with foreboding. When Paul was quiet, it was the quiet that held the force of a hurricane. Diego simply watched his brother in troubled silence.

"Paul," his father said softly, rising and coming over to him. "Paul, are you alright?" Paul shook himself awake.

"Forgive me, Father," he said dismally. "My mind isn't my own right now."

"You must be tired," his mother observed kindly. "Let me serve you, Paul." She ladled the savory stew into his bowl and gave him a bit of bread with butter and wine. Paul ate quietly for a short time but then put down his fork, his wine untouched.

"Father, forgive me, but I'm not very hungry," he apologized. "May I be excused?"

His father nodded with furrowed brow. "Maybe you ought to lie down," he suggested. Paul nodded. Rising, he entered the living room and sank down on the couch, staring into the flickering flames. His father watched him through the open doorway between the two rooms, and his concern grew. When the meal was finished, he went and sat beside his son.

"Paul?" he whispered, as his wife and oldest child slipped into the room, having herded the other children upstairs to play. Paul slowly stirred.

"Yes, Father?"

"Please tell me what's troubling you, son."

"There is a girl at the leper colony," Paul muttered, half to himself. "Her name is Iria. She's not even my age and she's only been there for a few weeks. She left home with her first cousin, Henry, as soon as she found she had the disease. Henry was one of the few people who didn't catch leprosy after coming to the camp. He was a nice fellow. . . I tried to find out why Iria's been so upset lately; I thought it was because of me. But Henry died this morning of cancer. I never thought I'd watch someone die – at least, not like that."

He dropped his head. Why was he so concerned for Iria now that she was alone? But she was strong; she'd be alright.

But he found himself voicing his concerns aloud to his father, with a strange hint of tenderness that slipped into his voice. Don Carreras looked, first sharply, then sympathetically at him and then at his mother, who also appeared to be moved. Paul sighed.

"You never saw anything like it, that fellow, Henry, dying; he was so good and brave, promising that girl that he would pray for her and everything . . ." Paul muttered.

His father watched him fondly for a few moments. "I understand now," he murmured. "Being close to death always makes a day darker. Henry sounds like he was quite a man, and it sounds like Iria needs a good friend, like you."

Paul nodded and tried to shake off the cloud that had settled so heavily over him. He looked around. He hadn't seen his baby sister for the better part of the last few weeks. "Is Imelda asleep already?"

"No, she's upstairs playing with Juan and Josef," his mother answered.

"May I be excused, then? I promised I would play with her."

His father gave him leave and Paul started up the stairs. Don Carreras watched him go and then shook his head, sighing.

"It has been a long time since I saw that side of him. He's learning to be gentle, but I hope that he can also learn that pain comes with any love. He's going to have a lot to face."

His wife nodded. "But clearly he has God's grace in him now," she said softly. "I think there will be nothing to fear."

IV

Illumination

The next day was Sunday, and Paul was allowed to stay home. He spent the day with his family and kept his mouth shut when tempted to grumble at attending Mass and the socializing afterward. He hated socializing, especially with the gabby older women who thought he was even more of a renegade than he prided himself upon being, and with the young men who looked down on him for being so wild. At least he had Imelda, whose sweetness always made up for the sour, lemon-like symptoms of such society.

It was that Sunday social that made him almost look forward to returning to the week's schedule. He didn't even wait for the Padre to arrive with the wagon; instead, he set off on his stallion, Rafael, the first time he had been allowed to ride the handsome creature since the beginning of his punishment. That punishment was still distasteful and terrifying for him: that bleak camp, those rags that hid the sickness of its inmates, and the sorrow and pain, mingled with a very quiet joy just barely able to be seen.

At least he would be able to check on Iria. He hoped she was doing alright. He knew from the death of his grandfather and one of his childhood friends that family was necessary to make it through grief. It was a hard thing for Iria to endure, for now she was truly isolated. She tried to amuse the children and soften their pains, and the pains of her fellow lepers, but somehow, she felt lost among them with her selflessness and loneliness.

Upon reaching the colony, Paul dismounted and ground-tied Rafael, giving him a pat on the nose and a piece of his favorite bread. He looked for Iria. It was a little earlier than he usually arrived. Most mornings he could find Iria doing her laundry, or perhaps praying down by the brook. But she was nowhere to be found, and the camp was quiet and still in the morning chill, wisps of fog rising from the stones. Paul moved through the courtyard, searching for the girl. He stopped abruptly upon rounding a corner at the far end where he had never set foot.

There was a cemetery; Iria knelt beside a fresh grave. The cross that stood there was simple and rugged. Paul choked as he watched the girl who bent silently over the cross. Tears sparkled in the sun as Iria placed a few happy wildflowers there in Henry's memory. A cool wind blew across the graveyard, scattering dead leaves and pebbles across the dusty ground and fluttering the flower petals.

Paul swallowed hard, running a hand through his thick, dark coppery-brown waves. Just as he had never been close to death, he had never been close to one whose grief was so great. Or if he had, he had never taken enough notice or given enough compassion. But now something seemed to be awakening him to reality and to the duties of his own heart. Why did Iria's isolation strike him so? She probably didn't think of him as a friend, not after how he had acted, but that didn't really matter if he could help her a little.

The youth removed his warm cloak of midnight velvet. Iria didn't hear him coming beside her. She was hugging herself, grasping a wooden rosary in one hand, which Paul had seen Henry praying with several times before. The youth stopped silently beside Iria as the sun wavered through the shadows cast by the trembling leaves of the slender uncertain trees planted there.

There was a moment of silence; then Paul gently draped his cloak over Iria's shoulders, tucking it closer about her as he knelt at her side. The girl looked up in confusion.

"You keep it," he muttered. "You need it more than I do."

Her eyes brightened slightly when she saw him and there was almost a smile, like a soft ray of sunlight. She nodded her thanks, for the tattered gown and robe she wore weren't warm enough to keep out the soft chill.

A heavy, supernatural feeling of sorrow briefly settled upon Paul's soul. What was this pain? Was it her pain? He shuddered a moment, realizing that God was putting the girl's sorrow in his soul. Why? What on earth was the point? But he softened as he looked at Iria again.

Her grief was multifaceted: she had lost her only friend, family, and protector she had with her, she was cut off from her family, and she was here to one day die of her illness. Paul, without knowing why, cast about for something to streng-then her in her trials.

He looked at the grave, and then at the flowers, whose petals trembled bravely in the breeze. "He loved you, you know," he whispered, surprised to hear his own voice. "And I . . . I think you should be proud of him. He died well, Iria, and I think that's more than most of us can say about anyone."

Iria nodded. Her veil fluttered and shook as it framed her face in shadows. She silently, almost numbly, marveled at Paul's sympathy but didn't wonder what it meant. She never judged if she could help it, and she almost wasn't surprised.

Paul's eyes landed on a little flowering plant, a slender, fragile stalk, bending in the weight of the wind, but whose flowers turned their faces bravely to the sun, despite the danger of being snapped in the strength of the breeze; they perched precariously upon the edge of a rock in the wall. Bravely, the plant defied the danger of its position, fought the likelihood of being crushed by the weather, and yet still blossomed. He frowned as he looked at it.

Iria followed his gaze and saw it, too, but she read the message in it better than he did. Even her namesake, the Virgin, had comforted her Son on the cross with a smile of love, though there was no joy in it. Iria nodded to herself and looked at Paul again.

A little smile tugged on her lips, and she held out her gloved hand. Paul hesitated. He was still terrified of close contact with any of the lepers, although he had already been assured that he wouldn't contract the disease that way. Like most of the population, he was likely immune. Like Henry.

Paul still hesitated. Iria touched his hand when he didn't move, and the boy jumped slightly but then swallowed hard and helped her to her feet. The girl gave him a soft, sad smile, and took her leave with a slight curtsy. Paul watched her go and wondered what had just happened.

~

As autumn breezed into winter, Paul grew accustomed to his work in the leper colony. He didn't mind playing with the children occasionally or aiding the adults in their chores. While his bad habits had slightly improved, his family still found many occasions to shake their heads at his doings.

As for Iria, she had begun to carry her cross in such a way that Paul couldn't help but admire her. She struggled and shed a tear or two in private as she wrestled with hope and tried to be certain that all was well with Henry and those she loved. The maiden embraced her selfless tendencies and almost lost her sorrow within her work caring for the other lepers.

Gradually, Paul found himself more and more easily distracted from his own thoughts by Iria's merry laughter as the children played, and he smiled more and more readily at the sound. He tried to make an excuse to himself but knew that there was none. He let it be.

It was December, the fourth month of his punishment, when he bumped into Iria as she was fetching water. It had snowed heavily overnight, covering the rocky terrain with white, and the brook had iced over. Paul gave the girl a smile.

"God's morning, Iria!" She smiled up at him.

"God's morning, Paul. Are you well?"

"As well as ever," Paul said shyly. This question from the lepers always made him wonder how to answer. How do you answer someone whose life is spent slowly dying?

Iria must have read his thoughts, and she laughed. "Even you, Paul, even you must admit every moment you are closer to your end. We aren't so different. Tell me, how are your little sisters?"

"Very well, thank you," he answered, beginning to smile again, crouching down beside her and inspecting the rocks at the water's edge. "Imelda lost her first tooth last night; I never realized how small and perfect baby teeth are."

Iria smiled, looking at the shimmering ice. "The strangest things are perfect, even in their imperfections," she murmured.

"Need me to break the ice for you?" Paul inquired with a grin.

"Always," she laughed.

Paul obligingly grabbed the nearest rock and hammered at it into the ice until he was able to create a hole big enough for Iria to dip her bucket in. As the frozen water spilled into her pail, Paul dug his gloved hand idly into the snowbank and found it to be perfect. His eyes twinkled with their accustomed mischief, and he watched Iria until she had taken her fill of the water and stood.

"Better let me carry that," he offered sweetly. Iria's expression seemed surprised, but she only gave the bucket to him with a thank-you and turned to lead the way to the communal firepit, where the water was needed to make stew for the evening meal.

A splatter of cold across her cloaked shoulders broke the ice of Paul's unusual sweetness. Iria whirled and hurled a snowball back at the laughing youth. It struck him squarely in the chest and he grabbed for more. Iria jumped behind the nearest boulder as Paul sent another snowball her way. Their merry laughter as the snowballs flew brought the children running, and they joined in the fun. Soon, no one was safe. Iria was hit in the side and she stumbled, nearly falling into the hole that Paul had made in the ice. Thankfully, the youth caught her not a moment too soon.

"Terribly sorry! Do you surrender?" he teased. Iria smiled a trifle faintly and nodded. Paul's smile faded. Had there been an unseen piece of ice in the snowball he had thrown? He looked into the girl's eyes and saw a flash of pain there, and she seemed all the sudden weary. Why did he feel that flash of pain too, but as a flash of fear?

"Are you alright, Iria? Did I hurt you?"

The girl nodded at first, then quickly shook her head at the second question. "No, it wasn't you," she breathed. "I haven't been feeling well all morning, I just tried not to show it because. . . well they always say not to show suffering, but I guess it just hit me hard at the same time as you did. I'm just tired I think. . . ."

"If you don't show suffering, how is anyone going to help you?" Paul scoffed at the idea. "I'm sure they only intend you to not make a show of it or use it to get attention."

Iria turned her eyes on him with a breathless smile that told him he was right, for once. But she swayed a little on her feet. Paul, seeing that she was on the verge of fainting, picked her up and carried her to the nearest cave and seated her by the crackling fire. The only other occupant now was another maiden, who was mending one of the children's tunics. Iria continued to keep an eye on the children, as was her duty when they played, but Paul's eyes didn't leave her.

"Iria, shall I keep an eye on the children for you?" he asked at last. "You need better rest than this."

Iria gave him a light-hearted smile. "Thank you, Paul, I'm feeling better now. I slept poorly last night and haven't eaten as much as I should have. It's my fault, as you can see."

"That could do it," Paul agreed with a laugh, though he wasn't entirely certain of that. He shook the feeling off, annoyed by his own anxiety. "I think we should rectify the latter issue. Shall I get something for you to eat?"

"Oh, I don't want you to go to the trouble–"

"Certainly not," the youth answered cheerfully. "That's what I am here for – helping, I mean, not just getting you lunch."

Iria laughed. "Thank you, Paul, but don't forget to be helping the Padre!"

Paul pretended to be annoyed at the reminder but scrambled to his feet and went to fetch something for her to eat. He returned a few minutes later with a stash of food they had brought from town.

"Here," he said cheerfully. "Marietta was getting lunch for everyone, so here's enough for both of us, and more. The Padre wants me to keep an eye on you and the children, so here I am."

He sat down and spread out a napkin on which he divided the victuals. There was a loaf of dark bread, two rounds of cheese, apples and honey, eggs, and an onion tart, warmed by the fire. Iria thanked him, and they began to eat.

"How have you been?" Paul asked abruptly, breaking a piece of bread and stuffing it with cheese. "Without Henry—I mean."

Iria took a deep breath and didn't look at him for a moment. She almost didn't answer, but with Paul's observation about suffering, she finally admitted that she was hiding her pain.

"Everyone needs me," she told him with downcast eyes so he would not see the tears that could not help but appear there as she spoke. "And . . . men always seem to think little of women when they cry, so I try not to." She paused to try to avoid the sob that came. "But it hurts so much, I don't have anyone now, just Jesus and Mary," she added softly. "Sometimes it's hard when you don't have someone who can hold you, who you can lean on."

Iria nervously began tearing her bread into pieces. She had hardly eaten anything. Paul's eyes couldn't help but see that she was hiding even more than she was saying. *Why did he feel like crying now?*

"Iria – I don't think that way about you. There's nothing wrong with tears of pain or love, even, only with crying over any little thing without a reason behind it. Men don't always discern between the two. I guess we don't see very well because we don't feel or understand quite as much as you," he said with a little laugh. "We tend to keep our tears inside and only in words, so you do the crying for us."

Iria didn't answer. Hesitantly, he stretched out his hand. "And as long as I'm coming here, you can lean on me," he said shyly. Iria looked up in surprise. She studied his eyes and then she smiled and took the hand he offered.

"Thank you, Paul! You are a good friend," she whispered.

"And good friends don't let their friends willingly starve themselves," the youth said quickly. "Will you please eat, for goodness' sakes?"

Iria laughed and obediently began to eat her portion of the onion tart. "Paul," she said finally, "I've been noticing. . . that you are a better man than I thought you were – I mean, better than before–" she stopped, embarrassed. Paul laughed ruefully and ran his fingers through his hair.

"You mean, reckless, rebellious, and rude? That's what everyone tells me."

"No," she murmured. "You aren't that now, Paul. Not as much as you were, at least. You have been growing much gentler, especially with the little ones. They love you, Paul. I think innocence is attracted to you."

Paul choked on a piece of apple. He looked at her soberly. "Iria, I've been far worse than you think. If innocence is attracted to me, that's a bad thing."

Iria gave him a gentle smile. "No, Paul. It doesn't matter what you *were*; it matters what you *are*." She gathered up the napkins and left him to ponder.

Paul stared after her, the dripping honey-apple in his hand forgotten. He felt his heart jump twice and a feeling he had never known came over him: sweet and clear like running water, gentle like spring rain, and lovelier than all the roses and irises in Spain.

V

Vexation

Morning after morning found Dona Rosita staring out the window in amazement as her son, not a moment late, ran out the door to meet the Padre before he had reached the door. Don Carreras was amazed to find that the mysterious vanishing of wine from the cellars slowed quite a bit; Marina was confused when Imelda came to her crying for playtime, for her 'Angel' said she should have more than one playmate. Diego was pleased when he found that Paul hadn't stolen his horse after Mass one morning, as was Paul's usual custom.

Juan and Josef, on one of their increasingly more frequent spying escapades, came upon Paul pacing like a tiger in the garden, pulling roses from the vines and tearing the petals apart. He cast them thoughtlessly on the ground as he went, leaving a pink carpet before the statue of the Madonna. The twins looked at each other.

"Are you thinking what I'm thinking?"

"You're definitely right," Josef replied, and they beelined off to Marina with the tale that Paul was hopelessly in love with a beautiful señorita and that she *must* find out the name, for clearly their brother was tormented by not being able to face the lady, whoever she was.

Marina, in the utter confusion and excitement that such news brings, especially with such a brother as hers, hurried to talk to him but ran into Diego instead. Diego wasn't so enthusiastic; he was rightly worried that this potential, probably phantom señorita, was not likely to be quite a lady, or if she was, Paul was destined for a heartbreak and a crash in the nearest tavern. Or his father's wine cellar. Either of which would land him in quite a predicament, knowing his history.

Diego, having finally convinced Marina to say nothing and merely to observe Paul, who would likely return to an unfortunate normal in the next week or two, promptly took his concerns to his mother.

Dona Rosita agreed with his sentiments, but she kept to herself the belief that something of love or its kind was wrong with her rebellious son. She, in turn, spoke to Don Carreras, who agreed wholeheartedly that they should watch Paul carefully and be understanding of him.

Aggravating him, in whatever state he was in, would make matters worse. He echoed his own words, saying that 'no lady in her right mind would marry Paul as he was.' He suggested that it was a greater progress in God's grace, that they had already seen in him after Henry's death.

His wife, in the mysterious way of a mother, believed that it was both great loves that were torturing her son, and she was right. But Don Carreras also knew, and hoped, that whatever love was bothering Paul would help him to tame his wild side, for there was certainly no better cure on the horizon.

So, Don Carreras and Dona Rosita wisely left Paul alone, treating his relapses with patience. Diego was content to watch and Marina, to worry and dream; but Juan and Josef were less easily persuaded to be calm. They loved to tease and prank everyone but most especially Paul, whose reaction was always most amusing. The twins did their best to discover the name of the supposed secret señorita.

First, they tried coaxing, then bribing to help him get cookies from the kitchen and wine from the cellar. To these first attempts, Paul just raised an eyebrow and looked mildly annoyed, before shaking it off and returning to his own business. But when they brought it up at the dinner table, he looked outraged. He let out his breath with a sigh when everyone else shushed the pair, leaving only Imelda looking confused.

Unfortunately, that accomplished the twins' designs: now they had a third accomplice. Imelda's curiosity and cuteness had always succeeded in getting answers from Paul whenever the twins had a mission, and they were sure this would be no exception. But it became a failure. Not innocent Imelda's cuteness, however. She clambered up onto Paul as he was flopped on the garden bench, trying to piece together a broken cross he had found in his room.

"Angel, Angel," she begged. "Want to tell me about the beautiful señorita?"

Paul started laughing as he looked up into her hazel eyes, surrounded by a halo of bouncing gold curls.

"What, the señorita your brothers have been imagining? There isn't one, unless it's you," he teased, tugging on one of her curls and making it bounce into her nose, leaving her in a fit of giggles. That spelled the end of using Imelda to find the answer, because she became absorbed in having a play-date with her favorite brother.

Then the boys tried their wiliest trick yet, and it was the simplest. They grabbed a piece of paper, bound it up with an old ribbon, and came flying into the house.

"Paul, Paul!" they yelled. Paul was coming down the stairs and stopped, wondering what they were about to do to him now. "It's from the señorita, and they said it's awful urgent! Must be sick or something!"

Without thinking, Paul jumped down the stairs and snatched the paper in his panic. A letter from Iria could only mean something terrible. But when he tore off the ribbon, he found the page blank and knew his brothers had gotten confirmation from him.

Furious, he crushed the paper and flung it at the twins. It bounced off Josef's head but only their mother's entrance stopped their cackling.

"If that had been who I thought it was, she'd have been dying," Paul snarled at his brothers. Dona Rosita took both twins by the shoulders and reprimanded them for their cruelty.

"Making someone think one they care about is in peril is no laughing matter," she said. "Your father will help you learn this." She sent the twins go off to their father to be lectured.

Paul waited to see what was in store for him, but it was only a smile and a kiss before he was allowed to go down to the garden and pace feverishly.

What no one realized was the torture he felt inside. It wasn't just his feelings for Iria. In ascending the ladder of virtue, one inevitably finds that some rungs are broken and others sharply splintered. Paul was beginning to feel his desperation to change and be the man everyone hoped for, and the one whom God had died for. Try as he might, every time he made good something always dragged him down again.

Temptations beset him left and right and scrupulosity ravaged his heart with a lion's bite. He couldn't go to confession for the thunderclouds that blinded him and threatened to burn him down when he tried to examine his conscience. He tried to pray, but dark thoughts beset him and tried to turn each word to impiety. He ran the rosary through his fingers but didn't dare say a word. Instead, he begged in silence to be delivered from the dark fog that seemed to enshroud his soul, while no one could see what he was going through.

Outwardly all was well, and he played with Imelda, teased his brothers, and spent his working hours with Iria and the children. Inwardly, he felt abandoned, for every time he trusted he would be answered, nothing came. As he watched

Iria in her gentleness and self-sacrifice, a chasm seemed to open between them and widen.

Disease, despair, and death all stood in his way. He watched that creature and didn't try to seal its gaping mouth. He was hopeless. The light that even sorrowful Iria held wouldn't come close to him. He wasn't good enough for her friendship if he couldn't change, couldn't die, couldn't live!

VI

Absolution

The next two weeks of Advent were spent rebuilding the little chapel, which was growing cramped and cold in the winter weather. The men worked hard to assemble the little building, while the women worked to keep them fed and well supplied with hot drinks and warm clothes. Iria had her duties with the children while Paul was recruited as a carpenter, as Father Bruno knew of his woodworking skills.

With every stroke of his knife and every blow of a hammer, Paul's pain went into that wood as though it were his own cross. The day was so busy, and the weather so cold, that Iria remained in the caves much of the day, and Paul never had the chance to catch a glimpse of her. Even if he had, it would have sent him into an abyss of deathlike torture inside.

When Paul's carving skills were noticed, he was given a block of wood and requested to carve a suitable image of the Blessed Virgin for the chapel, for the last one had been struck in a recent thunderstorm and had burned away. The perplexed youth took up a workspace in the cave given to him with a view of the brook. His fingers trembled when he tried to carve, for he feared the thoughts that would come to haunt him and harm the sweet lady whom he was trying to envision.

But the deeper his blade drove into the wood, the more peace and concentration he seemed to find, and an image of the Lady of Valencia, Mother of the Forsaken, soon began to appear before his eyes.

Madre mia, don't forsake the one who has forsaken you.

"Oh!" a soft gasp interrupted his work one hour, and he jumped to find Iria at his side.

"Oh, Paul, in truth your skills are wonderful," the girl breathed, as Paul felt a mix of joy at her approval, and pain at her presence. "She is ever *so* beautiful. I always loved visiting her so often. . . ."

She tilted her head slightly as she found the tears that Paul had unknowingly marked upon the Queen's face. "You made her cry," she said softly. Iria turned her eyes to Paul's face. He pretended not to notice the look and concentrate on the image before him. "May I show you something?" the girl broke the moment's silence.

Paul flung down his tools with a sigh and obediently followed her out into the sunlight. It was warm that day, and the snow had melted. The brook had flooded its banks and seemed to bubble more musically than ever. A sweet breeze blew through the empty branches of the little trees in the vale and brushed their faces. Iria closed her eyes with a soft breath of contentment. Paul saw all the weariness fade from her lips, and now it was his turn to cock his head.

"You like the wind then?"

Iria nodded and opened her eyes. "This is what I wanted you to know. The wind was always special to Henry and me." She smiled at the memories. "My mother told us that the wind is God's way of holding us, and teasing us, too. I suppose because it's invisible like He is, yet you can feel it and still see its effects. . ."

She watched the clouds being breathed across the sky. "Henry always said it was the Holy Spirit. Every time I'm anxious or worried, I feel a breeze, even if there was no wind a moment before, and I know He's trying to make me smile."

She turned to him, half-apologetically. "I thought maybe it would help you to think of Him when you feel the wind. . . if you're hurting, maybe He'll do the same for you."

Paul didn't answer but watched as a few dead leaves were scattered across the stone, and suddenly a haze of purple seemed to carpet the ground, as the wind tore the petals of an iris and pooled them at his feet. They seemed to hasten back to him a memory of Imelda's birth and the flurry of fear that she might be lost at any minute; but irises had carpeted the ground the next morning, and his mother, pointing, whispered softly that irises were made for hope, for hearts full of thorns and fear. Imelda ever echoed her mother's words whenever she caught a glimpse of her special flowers.

A smile came to his lips then without him realizing it. He gathered the ruffled petals and put them in Iria's hand.

"Reminds me of you," he said briefly and returned to his work with some solace.

True to Iria's words, he began to find that when despair seemed to swallow his soul, or pain flood his heart, or rebelliousness hold sway, the wind brushed his cheek and tousled his hair.

Similarly, Dona Rosita began finding yellow flowers blooming whenever she prayed for her son and the torture he had finally confessed to her.

At last, the chapel came together, and when Paul came home early one night, aching and tired, he was only too happy to tell his family all about it. The side walls were made of rocks cemented together, and the roof was of timber from trees that grew a few hundred yards outside the camp. The cross erected on top was carved of wood, while the altar was built of carefully carven stone. Two niches had been carved out of the rock wall on either side of it, inside of which stood two statues, Paul's statue of Our Lady, and one of St. Joseph, hand-carved by the youths.

A few benches, enough to seat all the lepers, had been put together with timber and rock. Father Bruno had brought candles and a crucifix. The women had placed bunches of wildflowers at the feet of the statues, garlands about the altar, and woven an altar cloth which made the chapel beautiful. Perhaps it was rough, but they were all proud of it.

Paul's brothers stared at him open-mouthed as they listened to his descriptions and his embarrassed confession that he had been the one to carve the beautiful wooden figure of Mary.

"I wish we could go there," Marina sighed. "It sounds nice."

"Me, too!" Imelda squealed happily, banging her spoon on the table. Everyone laughed.

"Sorry, baby sister," Paul answered, going around to the other side of the table, scooping her up and tickling her. "You would have to stay home; you know you get sick easily." Imelda pouted thoughtfully, then her face lit up with an idea.

"If I got sick, then I could be with you all the time!" Their parents chuckled softly, but no more was said on the subject.

After dinner, Paul kept his promise to play with Imelda and took her out into the sunset garden, where she made dolls and turtles out of pansy petals and ivy leaves. She wouldn't take any of the other flowers from the garden for her dolls; she wanted everyone to be purple and green.

"Purple is best," she confided to him, "because it's for me. I'm watching for the irises, 'cause then I know it's almost my birthday!"

"Mm," Paul said and tickled her nose with a marigold blossom. "I saw one this morning. You tell me every time you see one, alright?" She nodded solemnly but wanted to know why.

"Because you're my favorite person in the whole wide world," Paul teased and wouldn't let her escape from the newest addition to her doll family, Señorita Pansy the purple turtle.

To his confusion, every day when he found himself thinking of Iria, he'd glimpse an iris blooming somewhere unnoticed, even through the snow. When he came home and was tortured by the thought of the maiden, Imelda would come scrambling into his lap and tell of the iris she had seen that day.

After Mass one Sunday, the child came flying up to him during the dreaded social, clutching a handful of bright blooms. "Angel, Angel!" she cried, but faltered and tumbled into the snow. Paul caught her up and seeing her white cheeks, begged to know if she were alright. She blinked and giggled. "The irises wanted a kiss," she said, but she was pressing them to her heart. She let him carry her home.

Paul found himself more often standing and watching the wind and the wild, and to his amazement he found that peace crept back in at times, until one blustery, sunny afternoon sent him away from the others. He found a moss-covered boulder for a seat and looked up into the cloudy sky.

Surely, the God who loved him so tenderly as to comfort him in his sinner's despair could not be so terrible to face. He couldn't be the one that made the confessional such a terrible, scrupulous crucifixion. What was it that forced him away? What the roots of his many terrors and sins?

And he found that he was terrified of making up the number of times that he had sinned; but remembered whenever he hadn't known how many times, he had never been punished for the lack of a number. Perhaps it was preferable to the terror that he might lessen the number, or increase it beyond reality. An estimate would be alright, or if he only said, 'many times,' or 'a few.'

He worried about taking too much time when there were others behind him, and of confessing sins that sounded inane. Well, the priest was there for him, and wasn't concerned about the length of time, and every sin had been heard before.

Some people confessed too loudly while he sat in line; well, he could cover his ears. Looking as dumb as he felt was better than adding to his list.

If his contrition didn't seem to exist, and he had done what he could to elicit it, if he willed to be contrite and make amends, then that was the important thing.

If he remembered a sin during the absolution, he could add it then, and the Padre was never annoyed. He had been promised that the Holy Spirit would never let him forget a mortal sin in the confessional, at least if he had searched his conscience well, so if he only remembered after his exit he did not need to fear.

Paul came to the gravest worry on his mind, the one that had seemed most unsurpassable. Now that he was being held so accountable for his faults, every slightest sin seemed like a mortal wound to his soul. He could never go to Communion, and whenever anyone spoke to him, he felt as though he ought to be in a grave, unworthy of anyone's attention especially when his family praised his improvements, and Iria gave him a smile. The pit that had seemed to be shrinking away began to grow again as Paul looked down at the ground. A sudden rush of the breeze, and a hand lightly touched his cloak.

"Are you well?" Iria's soft voice came.

Paul jumped. "I wish you wouldn't do that," he said, with a little laugh.

"I'm sorry, I was trying not to startle you too much since you were so deep in thought."

"It's alright." Paul looked down at the ground again. The wind filled the silence for a few moments, but strangely, Iria's hand didn't leave his shoulder.

"How do you know if a sin kills your soul, Iria," Paul asked abruptly. "If it were a wound, you would never question the amount of blood."

"It is more subtle, isn't it," she murmured. "But. . . if you well and truly question whether your sin is mortal, not merely because you wish it not to be, then it probably isn't; for you would have to know in the first place as you do it that it is mortal, and that it truly is, and desire it entirely." She looked down at him, her face, as always, half lost in the shade of her veil. "You doubt your own heart too greatly, Paul," she said. "Go to the Padre, please."

With a last comforting glance, she left him. As he looked up a moment too late, not all the rain in Spain could wash away the scent of irises left in her wake.

The next morning's rainstorm found the journey to the leper camp delayed, but found Paul kneeling in the greystone church. The Padre had been dragged to the confessional, albeit not unwillingly.

Doubt, oh what doubt! Iria had confirmed his thoughts. If his heart was not to be doubted, then oh, what else should he not doubt? What was proven now, that he had believed to be a fool's thought!

As he arose and looked upon the tabernacle, his heart sang with a joy and love and freedom he had never known before. Oh, that his God was such a God, the true God, and that He loved him so much that all the pain and torment brought Him closer in the kiss of friendship, and no chasm could keep them apart. Paul could no longer feel that God was distant, nor a wrathful Judge. If the wind was to comfort him in his sinfulness, God was truly Father, and Brother, and Friend!

Paul found himself smiling as he prayed his penance, unaware that the Padre could not help but stand and watch him with the joy of the father of the prodigal son.

"O heavenly Father!" Paul breathed, heart locked in the tabernacle. "Please let it be true that I shouldn't doubt myself the way I have. If one heart brings another to You . . . I feel that no matter its fate and future pain, mine was made for hers, and I can be there for her as she has been for me."

Paul was beginning to understand that no matter Iria's fate, his heart was meant to love her. This was all that mattered. Not her disease, nor any ridicule or suffering to follow. A flash of fear made him doubt that he could avoid committing his sins again, but he raised his eyes again and begged for help. This time, his resolutions were not in vain. God would help him to accept his failures and make of them an offering, and He would help him to be the one He had made eighteen years ago.

"Paul?" The Padre's voice broke in softly. The young man looked up quickly, unperturbed by the interruption.

"Yes?"

"It's getting late; I think despite the rain I'll make ready the wagon. Will you be ready to leave soon?"

Paul arose. "I'm ready right now," he assured the priest. "I'll be taking Rafael, since I rode him here." Padre Bruno looked Paul up and down for a moment, smiling.

"If you don't mind getting wet, I'll save you from confessing impatience at your next confession and give you leave to go on ahead." He was laughing as he spoke, as though he could sense the boy's thoughts.

Paul laughed easily and didn't turn down the offer. He didn't know that it was the last day of his punishment. His mind, heart, and soul had been so deeply entangled the past five months that he had almost forgotten that it was a penance. But even the cold of the rainstorm was no penance!

Greatly amused at the prospect of the long ride through the rain, Paul pulled his cloak closer around him and swung onto Rafael, grateful that his horse had no preference for the weather. All around was a shroud of silver as he rode on through the stony landscape, that, come the morrow, would blossom with flowers and become a rustic Eden in its own right.

The sun was peeking through the rain, lighting each drop like a star-fallen diamond, as Paul dismounted Rafael and dashed into the nearest cave. The stallion trotted in after him, much to the delight of the children who were waiting for the rain to stop. Paul pushed back his hood and shook his damp hair out of his eyes. His ample cloak had caught most of the rainwater, but he was glad to sit by the crackling fire and have Rafael do a few tricks for the children.

". . . Paul? Paaaaaul!" a voice came ringing into the cave. Paul hastened to the entrance, and Iria nearly collided with him, completely drenched. She didn't seem to have noticed. "Paul!" she exclaimed with delight, seizing his hand with her gloved one. "Come quickly!"

With no further ado, she dragged him, cloakless and laughing, out into the rain. The sun was arching overhead now, and the clouds were barely an iridescent mist over the dome of the sky as the rain continued to fall. The dust had turned to mud in the cemetery, but wildflowers and grasses were nodding to the beat of the raindrops.

Iria pulled Paul to the foot of Henry's grave. Overnight, a dozen irises had sprung from seed and carpeted his resting place with blossoms of purple, white, and gold, and a creeping vine with the leaves of a rose curled over the cross at his head. Buds that sparkled with pearl-like drops promised to bloom soon. Iria turned to Paul, and he realized that tears were mingling with the rain.

"He promised," she choked. "He waited – until you had helped me trust, and be brave without him." Her mantle slipped from her head as she looked up at the clouds. "And – he sent me God's smile!"

Paul followed her gaze and saw what it was that had pulled her out into the rain. An archway of color spilled across the sky, framed by frothy golden-blue and white. That path to Heaven had never been seen in such colors, radiant like sunlit gems, shimmering with the icy clouds that passed before them. It seemed to rise from one end of the valley to the sea, many, many miles away. The birds were singing now and it couldn't have been a more fitting song.

Iria had no more cause to worry over Henry! Her faith, her love, her selflessness was finally rewarded by the promise Henry had made. The pain of his death was healed, and Paul felt his heart swelling with joy, for this rainbow was the answer to his prayers, too, that he might not fall again under the dreadful deluge of temptation.

"Oh, 'Ria!" he sighed, and turned to look at the maiden whose heart was busy singing. An impulse made him gently fold back the hem of the veil that always shadowed her face.

"Why, you have a rainbow smile like Imelda!" Paul breathed wonderingly. He touched her shoulders and gently pulled her into his arms. Iria's smile faltered.

"Paul, no, please," she whispered fearfully. "Please, you're going to get sick–"

"Ssh," he soothed her. "I may be reckless, but you can trust me this time. . . I promise. Without you, Iria, I was lost, and always would have been. I need you more than you know, and so God made my heart for you. Whatever happens now, Iria, I will *always* be here for you."

Iria looked into his eyes, so clear and tender, and knew her heart could not argue with him. Full of fright, she turned her eyes to the rainbow and grabbed Paul's arm.

"Oh, look!" she gasped. A second arch now glowed above the first, to answer her terror. Far less could she argue with it than with Paul's recklessness. She turned back to him, the adrenaline fading, leaving her trembling. Her shaky breath softly touched Paul's cheek as he enfolded her in his arms again and gently kissed her scarred brow. Iria closed her tear-filled eyes and finally let her head rest on his heart.

The rain softened, and pattered on, embracing them both and sinking into dust beneath their feet. They didn't hear the Padre drive into the camp. He saw them and said nothing, only turned, smiling at the God whose smile crossed the sky.

VII

Desperation

"Mother?" Paul called cheerfully, throwing the door open. It was early afternoon on a Friday, and the Padre had given him a half day so that the boy could work on his birthday gift for Imelda. Her birthday was that Sunday. Even though it was now Lent, they would still celebrate a bit. Paul thought of the little statue of Mary he was carving for her, as he checked through the house.

It was strangely silent. Where was everyone? Then he realized how dark the house was as well. All the shutters were closed and the curtains drawn. Paul felt a chill of fear. In his family, this was always done when there was some threat of tragedy afoot, some malady that was somehow hoped to be aided by the shade but not by the bright sun.

Paul felt a cry for his mother rising in his throat, but he had to stop it – shouting wouldn't help whoever was ill. He ran up the stairs to the bedrooms, taking the steps two at a time. The boy paused in the hallway down the length of which stretched, on the left, his parents' bedroom, Marina's, and the twins'; to his right was Diego's and the nursery. And it was outside the nursery that the twins sat huddled with their knees to their chests, as Marina and Diego at intervals exited the room and tried to comfort them.

"'Melda!" Paul cried involuntarily; his voice was soft enough to not carry into the room. Marina turned as she made to reenter the nursery.

"Paul!" she gasped. She flew into his arms for a moment, trying to smother the sob that seemed etched in her throat. "I tried – I couldn't do anything! The doctor's here now–"

Paul grasped her hand and pulled her into the room. His father and mother and Diego all glanced up distractedly. The curtains here, too, were drawn, but left a panel of light to softly illuminate the little bed. Candles glowed against the walls as a doctor clothed in black stooped over Imelda. Her golden curls were strewn over the pillow, her face white as her chest rose and fell too rapidly with her little gasps for air.

"Daddy – hurts–" Imelda whimpered, trying not to cry.

"I know, sweeting," he murmured with a pained look as he held her tiny hand. "But the doctor is going to help you, and you're going to be alright."

"'Melda?" Paul whispered, unable to hang back with Marina any longer. Imelda heard him and turned her head to try and see him.

"Angel?"

Don Carreras stepped back, and Paul dropped beside the bed to look into his little sister's anxious eyes.

"Oh, poppet, what's the matter with you precious?" he breathed, kissing her cheek as the doctor straightened and turned away.

"The moon – medicine – didn't work, Angel," she said, gulping. "I don't want to be sick, 'cause everyone is scared, but God wants me to be sick so I have to." Her hazel eyes looked very big as she lay there, looking at him. "Am I going to die, Angel?"

Paul choked and gently squeezed her tiny fingers. "He hasn't told me that. But I'm going to talk to Him, and He's going to take care of you."

Imelda shook her head. "Can't make Him say yes, Angel – maybe He wants a hug, and I'll give Him one for you, but you promise you'll be a good Angel all the time anyway?"

"What," Paul couldn't seem to stop choking. Where was the wind now, and where were the irises? It seemed the sky had faded to ash and smoke and all the flowers had died. But Imelda insisted, as she, too, began to choke, but it was the little heart in her chest that wasn't listening to her.

"Promise," he whispered, "but now you need to calm down and be quiet, precious, so your heart calms down too. Promise?" The child nodded weakly and sank back into the pillow mumbling for her mother. Dona Rosita took Paul's place and the doctor pulled him and the others aside.

"I'm afraid that my news is nothing but ill for you," he said gravely. "There's nothing that I can do for your daughter, Don Carreras. It will take a miracle for her heart to heal this time! But I can only suggest that she be moved, as quickly as possible, to the convent of the Poor Clares of the Holy Spirit in the hills. The quiet and the peace of God are all that I can recommend for her now . . . and you."

A sob escaped Marina's lips and Diego pressed her head to his shoulder. Why couldn't her healing skills have done something? Move her to the convent – no hope? How could one have peace without hope? She wanted to cry, not knowing that it was what each one of them struggled not to think.

Paul couldn't believe it. His heart was freezing in his chest. After such a beautiful time, how could it be that this was happening?

"Why," he said in pain, "why couldn't it have been me?"

"You weren't ready to die," his father said quietly.

". . . Imelda is the only one I've ever known who's always been ready," Diego sighed.

"I should have been able to do something," Marina whispered. She was wondering if it were her fault – she had always been able to help Imelda. Somehow, her passion for healing had always seemed to help when it seemed so impossible.

"It's not your fault," Diego murmured, stroking her hair. "If neither you nor the doctor can do anything, I doubt if anyone could, and God chose it that way."

Marina sighed, knowing he was right and trying to crush the guilt she felt. "She must go to the nuns right away. At least that might help. . . a little?"

"Yes, Diego, please, go tell the servants to ready the carriage and gather Imelda and your mother's things," Don Carreras bade. "Oh, would that I could leave! If only the town could relieve me for a week, a month – but no, send a message to Don Jiménez, he will be most willing to take them all the way to the convent."

Diego nodded, squeezed Marina's shoulders, and fled the room.

"Shall I be going, daddy?" Marina raised her eyes to her father's face. He touched her cheek.

"No, sweeting. . . I think I'm going to need you." She could feel his heart aching as deeply as her own.

Paul turned despairingly to his father. "I could go!" he said. "And why not Diego? Imelda needs us!"

"You wouldn't be allowed to stay with them at the convent, you know that, and you have nowhere to go in the hills but the snow," his father said gently. "Imelda will have your mother, whom she needs most, and God will see to them. We can't go, Paul, and we must find our places here . . . sometimes, it's in the pain and torture of leading our everyday lives with our everyday tasks."

"But – what if it's not an ordinary task?" Marina asked, her eyes suddenly brightening with hope. "Paul, the statue! For Imelda – you could go to Valencia!"

Paul opened his mouth to object in confusion and abruptly shut it again. "By your leave, father!" he exclaimed, kissed Imelda, and tore out of the nursery.

"Paul, where are you going?" Don Carreras exclaimed, as he stepped into the hall and almost collided with the youth, who was returning from his room. Paul, still chilled with fear, settled his winter cloak over his shoulders.

"I'm going to the Virgin in Valencia," he said softly. "I don't know if she'll help Imelda. But we'll need her to do something for us!"

"Paul, that's a two-day journey. I do hope you're taking more than a cloak?"

"I'll count it as a sacrifice," Paul replied.

"No, you'll count it as a bad case of pneumonia. You'll count it as a sacrifice to take what you need. Ah, Diego–" His eldest was returning up the hall. "Please see to it that Paul takes sensible items with him and leaves his recklessness at home."

Don Carreras vanished back into the nursery to sooth his crying child. Diego looked blankly at his brother.

"Valencia," Paul said briefly, and his brother understood.

In five minutes, his satchel had been packed and Rafael's saddlebags had been tended to. Loaves of bread, flasks of almond milk and hot herbal tea, salted bacon, dried fruits and cheeses, as well as a few instruments of protection and warmth and sustenance for Rafael, were the 'sensible' items his father had had in mind.

Paul felt as though he had a clock ticking in his head as he hurried from the kitchen. Dona Rosita was descending the stairs, Imelda bundled in her arms, as the door swung wide open. It was the Padre. Everyone stopped.

The priest took in the situation and laid his hand on Imelda's brow, but his eyes were just as tired as those of Don Carreras. "May God heal you, my little one," he murmured, and sent them outside. His eyes turned to Paul. *Why did the air seem to freeze again?*

"It is good that you're going, Paul," the priest said quietly. "I'm afraid. . . that Iria needs your prayers, too. She took a turn for the worse not long after you left."

"No!" Paul cried without a thought. He never knew afterward how he found himself on Rafael, if it was the entire room that had spun and spit him onto the stallion's back, or if it was only his head that had spun and he had somehow made it at a run. The frantic breath of desperation was upon him.

The sting of ice and on the wind brought him to as Rafael galloped through the snow. He must have been riding hard for nearly an hour, for the village was well out of sight. He pulled Rafael back into a trot. No matter his impatience, it would not aid either of them to spend their ride at full speed and frozen by the wind.

The wind? Paul paused and glanced upwards. Was it only the rush of the gallop, or was there a breeze? It was still now.

Paul shut his eyes and prayed. He prayed to the woman whose love for man was so sweet and ran so deep it brought God's wine to a wedding. There were no words that could form the intentions in his heart, not the desperation to save the two maids he loved most, not the terror of losing them, or the grief that would threaten to return him to the chasm of despair from which he had just been freed. Not the healing of the maiden he loved; oh, why couldn't he save her when she had saved him! Or the gift of a normal childhood to the sister he had always protected. Nor the strength and hope his family needed, nor the dire need to believe, to cling to something and not return to the days where he had walked without God and scorned Him.

He had to believe that there was love; he had to believe even if it was lost! And yet the words begging God to save them wouldn't come to his lips, because it wasn't his choice to make. And he feared it was not the choice God would make.

All was hope and love and light in Iria and Imelda. . . they deserved to be with God, and by it be healed of their illness. Who knew what would happen? Both could be lost, or neither, or only one, and a thousand effects upon them all.

"Oh, Madre, don't forsake us," were the only words that came to his numb lips. He had to force himself to believe in the love that he had felt so short a time ago. And then the breakneck pace began again. No snow or ice or highwaymen could stop him from reaching Valencia.

~

Hooves clattered on stone and a few men sprang out of the way as Paul and Rafael flew through the golden streets of Valencia. Rafael seemed to share his master's sense of urgency, or did he simply love to run? Despite the difficulties of travel, they had reached the city in good time. It was likely that his mother and Imelda had only just arrived at the convent.

Pulling his stallion to a flying halt at the foot of the cathedral, Paul looked about anxiously. He couldn't leave Rafael standing there. Spotting a young boy playing with his dog on the cathedral steps, Paul called to him and pressed a few coins into his hand. He begged the lad to find a place for Rafael to stay and be fed while he prayed. The child's eyes lit up, and he obediently took hold of Rafael's bridle and led him down the street.

Paul watched until they had left his view. Recklessly trusting that the boy was of good heart and would return to tell him where the stallion had been stabled, he slipped inside. High above the door was a latticed rose window, as though of deftly woven lace. Colored light shafted down softly through the arched and colonnaded nave of the church. It was cool and dim, and almost silent save for a few faint whispered prayers, the pealing of a bell, and somewhere, a hymn being chanted rhythmically.

The rush of the ride seemed to be catching up to Paul, for his eyes wanted to close. He wanted to find peace and rest from anxiety, but first he had to find the image of his Mother.

The gesture of such a journey with his pain, to speak to her and give his eyes some visible symbol of the one who loved him, would surely bring some grace, if not the healing they were all desperate for.

Forcing himself awake, Paul moved through the church, blending with the quietness of the haven as he made each movement as silent as was humanly possible. It was as though his soul strained to hear audibly, and his ears strained to hear what was found in silence. The smell of incense and burning candles lingered all about as Paul finally came upon the one he sought.

The scent of winter blossoms enveloped her image and candles flickered at her feet, causing the draped gown of gold and sky blue to shimmer. Her dark hair fell down her shouldders as she cradled her Son and a bouquet of silver lilies. She stooped forward, anticipating Paul's speechless request, her lips almost touching his brow, her hand almost ready to lie on his shoulder. Her brown eyes seemed to be alive as she looked into his eyes, and the Child did, too.

Paul didn't need to try to form the words in his heart. It might be only an image, an image made by the angels, but when he looked upon her, he knew his mother looked back.

"Ay, *Madrecita*! Aid the ones I love as you aided me when I had forsaken you!" he breathed, and took the kneeler before her.

~

He must have fallen asleep. Paul opened his eyes and started when he saw how low the candles had burned, and the light that cast soft shadows over his Mother's face. Paul scrambled to his feet, recalling that he didn't know where Rafael was. Somehow, that rest had taken away his anxiety, leaving him content with only a mild weariness deep inside.

Shaking his head to clear it of sleep, he took his leave of the Lady and hurried back through the nave. He ducked around a pillar and collided with a young man who must have been close to Diego's age.

"Forgive me!" they exclaimed together, and tried not to laugh as they picked themselves up. The stranger straightened his tunic and looked him up and down.

"You wouldn't happen to be the master of a black stallion by the name of Rafael, would you?"

Paul tried to place where he had seen eyes like this young man's. "How did you know?"

"A boy led him up to me in the street and handed me the reins, saying the beast needed a stable and I'd find the dark-haired young stranger in the cathedral," the man laughed. "Funny thing, too. I'd never seen that boy before, so I don't know how he knew I could care for your horse. But never mind! I had Rafael taken to my family's villa on the outskirts of the city. It's an inn of sorts. Come along, I'll take you there."

"Thank you," Paul said gratefully. "I'm Paul Carreras, by the way!"

They pushed open the great doors and came out into the bustling streets. Men and women were passing to and fro, and there were many shouts filling the air, for it was market day. Children were playing all throughout the plazas on either side of the church.

"I'm Fernando Ramirez," the young man called over the noise.

Paul snatched the youth's sleeve. Fernando jumped and was forced to turn around. Those eyes! They reminded him of Iria's, only darker.

"Do you have a sister?" he asked urgently.

"Don't tell me you're one of those types," Fernando replied, freeing himself and starting down the stairs.

"No! Do you have a sister named Iria?" Fernando went very still. His eyes slid back to Paul. Paul detected the sudden creeping pallor beneath Fernando's skin.

"How would you know?"

"I work in the leper camp," Paul said quietly. Now he knew that his suspicions were true. Iria had let slip the fact that she had frequently used to visit the image of the Lady of Valencia. After his healing, it been his intention to pursue the clue for her sake, but it had almost slipped his mind in the panic of the last few days. ". . . She's part of why I'm here."

Fernando drew a rattling breath, his face ashen now. "What do you mean," he hissed, grabbing Paul's shoulder.

"I mean. . . that she's taken a turn for the worse. . . and is too afraid to tell us where you are. She thinks it would be the death of you."

"I don't care what she thinks," Fernando snarled. "I'll take you to your horse, and then you take me to her!"

VIII

Retribution

"Iriaaa!" Fernando's impatient voice rang through the camp as he threw himself from his horse. The lepers glanced up in confusion at the sound of the newcomer. Paul jumped down from the saddle, anxiously sliding the reins over Rafael's head.

Fernando had explained why Iria was so adamant that her family not be contacted. When she was a child, she had fallen asleep in the family's chapel while the candles burned low; one of them had caught the garment of the Virgin's statue on fire, and before it could be stopped, the fire had spread through half the house. Fernando had rescued Iria, but had received severe burns in the process, as had his mother. The rest of the family had been out working in the fields and the stables and had escaped any injury. Iria had blamed herself for everything.

"Heaven knows why she did," Fernando had muttered, looking at the scar covering his forearm. "It would have happened regardless of who was in the chapel, if anyone. . . if she hadn't been in the chapel calling for us, we wouldn't have known about the fire in time. When she caught the illness, she believed it was punishment and proof of her guilt. But why, when the burn given to me could easily be for my sins and not for hers?"

Paul had seen the remnants of the fire's damage when they had retrieved Rafael from the villa. When Fernando's mother and father had asked in alarm the cause of their son's anxiety, they had intended, in equal desperation, to come along.

But Paul and Fernando had begged them to wait. Given Iria's reticence they knew the effect of Fernando's appearance would not be good. If mother and father came, too, she would panic that much more. They begged them to wait until they had seen her and convinced her that all was well. Only for their daughter's sake could Don Ramirez and Dona Maria resist the urge to go to her.

"Or for nothing," Paul had replied to Fernando, "when I've been far worse a case than anyone I know, and yet these illnesses of my sister and yours come only after my conversion." Fernando had only nodded and looked down the road, praying for the camp to arrive in view soon.

"Iria!" Fernando shouted again, running into the complex. Paul followed. His heart kept skipping beats, for he didn't know what Iria's condition was or where she was. She couldn't have been – no, she couldn't have been lost yet!

And then, as they rounded the bend, Paul saw the girl standing, panic-stricken, at the cemetery's edge, listening to the voice that was calling her name. When she saw for certain who it belonged to, she fled.

"Iria, no!" Fernando cried desperately.

"Wait!" Paul grabbed his arm and ran after Iria alone. Iria stumbled and fell before the entrance to her cave. She tried to pull herself to her feet, but she was too weak.

"Iria, oh Iria!" Paul gently caught her by her shoulders and lifted her up, shaking. He pulled her back against him.

"No, no Paul, I can't! I can't let him," she wept, her dark hair falling free from her veil.

"Iria, you can't run away this time," he whispered. "The risk is his to make, and he's chosen it. You aren't being punished, Iria, you're here because I needed you. . . we all needed you. The pain of separation is the deepest wound your family's hearts can hold, and you've *all* suffered for far too long . . . God isn't punishing you; can't you tell by the wind and the rain?" he breathed.

Iria tilted her head back against his shoulder; her eyes closed as tears continued to run down her cheeks. "I thought that's what He said, but I was too afraid," she whispered. "Oh Paul, if any of them come to live here because of me, I couldn't – I couldn't–"

"Yes, you could," he answered, turning her towards him. "I thought you trusted me, sweet." Iria looked up at him for a moment, her tears slowly dissipating. She sighed and pushed her hair beneath her mantle.

"I know you're right," she said, hushed and sad. Paul gently touched her face.

"Come then. . . your brother needs you as much as you need him now."

He put his arm around her, for she scarcely had any strength to walk. He set her down on the boulder where she loved to work in the mornings at sunrise.

Fernando was standing where he had been abandoned, hands clenched as he waited for his verdict. How he had held himself back, he didn't know. For a moment, Iria couldn't look at him; she raised her eyes at last. Brother and sister looked at each other for a few moments in pale silence. Iria broke down in tears and stretched out her hands towards him.

"'Nando!" she called.

Fernando responded to his release and swept his little sister into his arms, pressing her to his heart. Iria could scarcely breathe for tears.

"Hush, my little Iris, I'm here now!" Fernando whispered and didn't let go.

~

Paul found himself standing in the chapel, looking at the statue he had carved. There was a guilty feeling deep inside, quite wrongfully, that he had not lingered in Valencia for Imelda's sake. But he knew he had done right, and that the Lady had led him to do so. He prayed that it would do well for Imelda as well.

Fernando and Iria were still sitting outside. Iria was too weary to move much. When the boys had pressed her, she had told them what was wrong. She had taken a turn for the *worst*, not simply for worse. She had little strength now, and it was waning quickly. Her body had grown numb and could feel no sensation of touch. She had pulled away from Fernando when she had told them this.

"I can't feel when anyone touches me," she groaned. "Do you know what it's like, when you can't be touched, and then when someone takes down that wall to hold you and you can't feel it?"

She had pressed her hands against herself, shrinking away from both men. "It almost hurts worse. . . than not being touched. . . I feel like a ghost, and I'm fading away. . ."

Their instinct had been to hold her, but they hadn't dared touch her, for her pain was too real. But Iria had shaken it off as quickly as it had come.

"Never mind," she said, smiling. "There's no time for that now." She had asked then about her family, and Paul's; when she heard of Imelda, she went very pale and laid her hand on Paul's shoulder.

"I didn't realize how much pain you have. . .forgive me. I will offer up my suffering for her, and I pray that it will do some good. I know it will, if not for what we first hope. Sometimes, the second hope is the better one, to God. . ." Paul had only squeezed her hand lovingly in reply. Not that she could feel it.

The youth sighed and gently rubbed his fingers on the hand of the Virgin. He could do nothing for Imelda but leave his heart at Mary's feet. He could stay with Iria and do what he could for her. He didn't dare imagine that the worst could occur.

Without warning, Paul felt a nerve in his right arm grow cold as though with a spark of ice, and a cold feeling settled in his stomach the way it used to before confession. He tried to disperse the storm cloud that seemed to loom over him, but he couldn't seem to shake the feeling that something dire was about to occur. He abandoned the chapel and found Iria laughing at some childhood tale Fernando was telling.

The rattle of a cart rolling down the entrance's incline drew their attention. Father Bruno waved and laughed when the children came screaming out of the caves, clamoring to pet Naranja and Caballo, the two sturdy bays. The priest shooed them away until he had safely maneuvered the wagon around them and set the horses at rest. Once the children had acquired their weekly assortment of treats, and the adults were collecting the supplies, he came to the trio.

"How are you faring, little daughter?" he asked, gently taking Iria's hands and inspecting her face. The blue of her veins stood out clearly beneath the pallor of her skin.

"I'm growing used to being a ghost," she replied with a little smile and turned to Fernando. "Padre, this is my brother. Paul found him."

Father Bruno's anxious eyes brightened and he smiled at the young man. "Ah, I am happy." He shook Fernando's hand. "I hope you can stay," he said softly, aside. Fernando nodded.

"I will, Padre."

"And the rest of your family, little Iria, will you let them come see you?" the priest inquired. Iria hesitated and looked up at her brother.

"If you say no, we're all going to be frustrated with you, and our parents will certainly come anyway," Fernando declared. "So, say yes, little sister, so we don't have to upset you."

Iria shook her head, but she was smiling. "Then yes," she said, half to herself. "I do want to see them. . . again. . ." The way she said it didn't help the spirits of the men with her, and she must have realized it, for she quickly reassured them that she was feeling better with the end of her self-exile.

"You look tired, Father," she said tenderly. "You've been worrying too much."

"Aye, I suppose," the priest admitted. He was glancing up the incline from which he had come.

"And nervous," the maiden observed.

The priest laughed and turned back to her. "I thought I was being followed all the way from the village, but they would have caught up to me by now. And for their health," he said dryly, "they probably turned aside when they saw where I was going. *If* they were following me. They may have been headed to the hermitage in the desert. Several pilgrims have been passing that way lately for the monks' wisdom."

"As for wisdom," Iria smiled, "a wise priest once told me that you pray, hope, and don't worry. Now, why don't you listen to yourself?"

The Padre chuckled. He turned at last to Paul, to ask how well he was faring with the heavy stresses laid upon his heart. His eyes belied his concern. If the pain was too great, and the losses they feared came to pass, would Paul's fledgling soul hold up to it, or be drowned in the hurricane? Before he had the chance to speak, a cacophony of hoofbeats fell upon their ears accompanied by a shower of gravel and the scent of smoke. They all ducked.

"Well, well! If it isn't Paul!" a voice cried from above. It was dripping with scorn. So, this was why Paul had experienced that sudden feeling of looming dread. He jumped to his feet and whirled to face the intruders. High on the bluffs above them stood three men he knew well. They had been his comrades in roguery. Rodrigo, the ringleader, had been his closest friend from childhood.

"Evening, Rodrigo," Paul raised his voice with wary eyes. "What are you after?"

"Good evening, Paul," Rodrigo drawled. His chestnut hair fell over his forehead in impeccable waves, but the smile on his face was twisted. "We were just passing by, when the thought struck us to come and visit you." He glanced around with an air of contempt, and his eyes fell on the chapel. He laughed. "Why, is that a chapel? It looks like a stable to me."

"The first place of worship was a stable," Father Bruno said under his breath. The ringleader looked around thoughtfully as the lepers drew closer together, and the priest came up beside Paul. Both knew the three men, and glanced warily at each other before looking sternly again at them.

"From the looks of this place, there isn't much point in it being here," the leader said at last. He turned to his companions. "What do you think?"

"The same as you," a strong, handsome youth answered with laughing eyes.

The third member of the group was hardly more than a boy, and seemed not to fit in very well. His expression was rather troubled as he took in the scene before him and listened to his companions.

These latter two were Alexandre and Francisco Jiménez, the sons of Don Jiménez, who was escorting Dona Rosita and Imelda to the convent. Don and Dona Jiménez were godparents to both Paul and Marina, and as such he had grown up with their sons. It was to be confessed that Paul had been the one who dragged them into such a life as this, although for them, it was only on the side, whenever Rodrigo felt like bullying them.

Rodrigo smirked at Alexandre's answer and turning, vanished from view for a few moments. He reappeared with a well-lit torch in hand. Paul realized that the trio must have paused to build the fire before making their grand entrance. It was Rodrigo's style. . . and explained why their appearance had been delayed from Father Bruno's expectations.

"Rodrigo," Paul began in a warning tone. He had moved in front of Iria. Her hand was on his arm. By now, the lepers were all gathering at the mouths of the caves, equally as troubled as he.

"Now, don't you think they deserve a nicer home, Paul?" Rodrigo called down to him. "That's what I thought; now why don't you gather all your friends and tell them to leave the complex. Because if they don't. . . I'm going to have to burn it down for them. Come on now, Paul, do us all a favor!"

"Rodrigo, no!" Paul snapped.

Rodrigo's eyes darkened as he looked down at his friend. "Come on, Paul," he said quietly. "Don't you want to eradicate the germs of sin that has put your sister on her deathbed?"

"It wasn't leprosy; it was her heart!" Paul cried, gritting his teeth and wondering how to change Rodrigo's mind. He had learned from experience the youth's tenacity, and given his arrogant disposition, he wasn't sure if mere words could be of service.

"Ye-esss, and I'm certain the germs made it worse," Rodrigo rolled his eyes. "Start herding everyone, Paul."

Paul's breath came through his teeth with a hiss. "I'll go talk to him," he muttered to Father Bruno. He started up the incline. The priest turned and gently motioned for the men and women to sidle to the opposite end of the vale, just in case. Rodrigo met Paul halfway down the slope.

"Don't tell me," Paul sighed, "that you're doing this just to talk to me?"

"Is that what you think? Last I checked, your penance ended a couple of weeks ago," Rodrigo replied. "Which means, you've been purposely avoiding me now that you're no longer forbidden to see me. What's a fellow to do? But no." His eyes darkened looking at him.

"Paul, you must be going soft! It's about time you had a good time again, little brother, and I'm here to see that you do. Drinks, thievery – I have a plan for tonight, and your father will never need know about it," he said confidently.

"Ah, yes, unless I tell him about it," Paul said sarcastically.

"Which you won't, certainly."

"Which I will, verily," Paul retorted. "I want no part in your escapades, Rodrigo, and I wish you didn't either."

Rodrigo frowned and changed the subject. "Amapola's been asking after you."

Paul had almost forgotten the farm maid, daughter of the nearest barón, Esteban Diaz, and a rather misbehaved young girl. She frequently happened to be in the taverns whenever Paul and Rodrigo had their usual adventures, and had grown fond of them both, particularly Paul. This was probably due to his family's status and the stubborn curl that always fell across his forehead. Paul had always found her rather annoying, although her own golden curls were cute.

"Tell her I work in a leper camp," Paul said darkly. "I'm sure she'll vomit and finally leave me alone."

Rodrigo chuckled and shook his head. "I hope you do realize that the last time you were drunk you said you'd marry her. Seven months is a long time to avoid your betrothed."

The look of disbelieving disgust on Paul's face cracked him up.

"Well, it's better than marrying one of them, isn't it?" Rodrigo jerked his head in Iria's direction. "But don't worry! I'll get you out of this mess like I always do."

"Rodrigo," Paul sighed again, wondering why he had ever gotten himself into said mess. "Look, I'll see you at home and we can talk, but for now, please leave my friends in peace. Imelda's not their fault, and you shouldn't care anyway because you've never even met her."

"Any sister of yours is a sister of mine," Rodrigo growled. "I'm disappointed with you. You used to be an amusing companion. And everyone knows lepers are the worst of the worst and the farther they are from civilization, the better for everyone. The germs of sin travel on the air, too, and I'd bet anything they're the cause of every evil thing in the village right now."

"Like you," Paul retorted. "If you believe that, I don't see why you aren't a leper yourself. I'll say this one last time. *Get out.* Or I'll throw you out the same way I threw your last new 'friend' out of the bar for crushing on Marina."

"That's how it is, is it," Rodrigo said softly. His eyes glinted dangerously. "This isn't much thanks for all the things I've done for you, Paul. You're right. Our friendship is broken. And I have no reason to play well by you, do I? Save your precious camp if you can!"

"Rod–!" before Paul could even grab Rodrigo's wrist, the torch had been hurled onto the wooden chapel roof!

"Rodrigo!" Francisco cried in horror. Even Alexandre paled as the flames began to leap up.

"*Gertrude!*" Iria suddenly screamed. The youngest leper child had fallen asleep inside!

"I'll get her! Stay!" Fernando yelled, pushing Iria back as she jumped to her feet.

"Fernando, no!" she cried, as her brother vanished into the flames. She couldn't bear to see him disappear into a fire again!

"Iria!" Paul shouted, glimpsing her diving in after him. *She couldn't feel pain! She couldn't feel if the fire touched her skin!*

In this one moment that had passed, Rodrigo hurled his fist into Paul's jaw and threw him sliding down the incline.

"Adios!" Rodrigo said in fury. "I hope this camp burns to the ground the way our friendship has!" He leapt onto his mare and spurred her away from the now smoke-filled vale. Alexandre and Francisco paled and hesitated, but finally tore after him.

Paul picked himself up dizzily and ran, stumbling, towards the chapel.

"Paul, no!" Father Bruno caught his arm and pulled him back as the chapel emitted a horrible creak and a groan. An explosion of sparks, and the wooden beams of the roof crumpled!

Not a moment too soon, Fernando threw his sister through the doorway and himself after, Gertrude in his arms, as the chapel crashed down. Now the flames were threatening to creep through the arid camp and devour it bite by bite!

Paul snatched up Iria and pulled her to safety.

"O Lord, Thou knowest what is best for us, let this or that be done, as Thou shalt please. Give what Thou wilt, and how much Thou wilt, and when Thou wilt. Let this fire not destroy this home of your forsaken ones, who have nowhere left on this earth but here," Father Bruno whispered, as the lepers drew closer and watched as their refuge burnt down before their eyes.

There was a rumble of thunder. The gray clouds that had been darkening all that morning suddenly broke loose with the full fury of heaven. Sheets of raindrops fell so fast they hit like hail, bursting and steaming in the fire's wake. The overwhelming heat radiating from the chapel vanished into the chill of the storm as the dry wood soaked, and became drenched.

As swiftly as it had begun, so it ended. The rain softened to a comforting patter on the mud beneath their feet. The stone frame of the chapel remained, but the roof and all that was wooden within had burned away.

"So much for replacing the statue," one man sighed, thinking of the lightning strike that had burned the first.

"Which one?" asked Fernando, coughing. He still hadn't caught his breath. Little Gertrude was in her father's arms now.

"The Madonna," the man replied. "It always falls to an accident."

"I could have sworn I just saw her still standing," Fernando murmured. He turned away, anxious that his sister might have been injured.

Paul was still holding Iria, whose clothing, like Fernando's, was scorched and blackened with soot. If they thought she had looked fatigued upon their arrival, she was nothing short of fatally exhausted now. Fernando wisely chose not to scold her for dashing after him.

"We match," Iria smiled weakly and showed him her right arm. A patch of red and violet spread across her forearm, identical to his scar.

"Oh, Iria," her brother sighed.

Paul's fingers found the swelling bruise on his jaw. It was sinking in just how far Rodrigo had gone. "None of them will tell anyone," he heard himself muttering.

"You must tell your father what they have done," Father Bruno said quietly. "Am I wrong in guessing that they have more than this planned for this night?"

"No," Paul replied. "He said he had some plan of theft. But I can't go!" he groaned. "I can't leave Iria. I couldn't even stay with my own sister."

"Paul," Iria pleaded softly. Paul hadn't realized she had overheard. The maiden stretched out her hand and touched his heart. "You can't – you can't let them hurt anyone else, Paul," she said. "If he did this, even to you, he could do far worse. . . we can't let him lose himself again."

"She's right," the priest urged. "I fear that Rodrigo is almost lost to us. If he is your friend, Paul, you must try to stop him before he enters the precipice and takes Alexandre and Francisco with him."

"So much chaos," Paul moaned, closing his eyes and wondering whether there was anything else left that could possibly go wrong now. He opened his eyes and looked at the three. "I'll go," he said at last. "I'll be back as soon as I can. Take care of her."

"We will," Fernando answered. He squeezed Iria's shoulders.

"I'll see you again, Paul, I promise, so please don't worry," the maiden told him. "But please be careful. If he hit you, he could hurt you far more."

"Now, who's worrying?" Paul scolded. "I'll have Father and Diego with me, I'm certain, so don't trouble yourself. We don't want you wearing out the remainder of your nerves." He kissed her fingers.

"I won't," she said obediently.

"May God keep you, and may Our Lady shelter you beneath her mantle, Paul," Father Bruno blessed him. Paul bowed his head and found Rafael grazing on the outskirts of the camp. Swinging into the saddle, he knew he could lose no time between Rodrigo, Imelda, and Iria's fates. He couldn't juggle all three. Only God could.

IX

Rejection

Paul shoved the stallion into an all-out gallop and was soon streaking across open fields and meadows. The stars began to shine faintly and the sun inched down below the horizon. At last, Paul saw the lights of his home glowing comfortingly in the distance and pushed his steed into an even greater speed. In no time, he was jerking on the reins, and his steed plowed to a stop, kicking up dust.

"Father!" he called. "Diego!" He leapt from Rafael's back, trying to run but finding his hand caught in the reins. Jerking them off, he ran up the steps and crashed into the door, shoving it open and causing the twins to flip their bowls of stew in shock.

"Paul! What's wrong, son?" Don Carreras was already out of his chair. He grasped his son firmly by the shoulders to steady him.

"It's Rodrigo," Paul answered, gasping to catch his breath. "He burned down the chapel, trying to burn down the whole camp."

"And hit you, I take it," Don Carreras interjected, dampening a napkin in wine and pressing it lightly to Paul's bleeding jaw.

Paul winced as the stinging set in. "He thinks of me as a traitor. He got away with Alexandre and Francisco. He wanted me to join them on some piece of thievery he has planned tonight."

"He's may have done it by now, whatever it is," Diego said quietly, stepping around the table. "We should visit Dona Jiménez and see if her sons have returned."

"Rodrigo will be difficult. If I sentence my own son to working in a leper colony, what will I do to him?" Don Carreras sighed. "*Vamanos!*"

Within minutes, they were dismounting at the door of the city home of the Jiménez family. The boys took the stairs up to the front door two at a time and their father knocked impatiently, only to have the door jerked open by Dona Jiménez. Her delicate face was as pale as the waning moon and her honey-brown hair tumbled down in anxious strands.

"My sons!" she said. "Have you come to get them, Juan?" Seeing that the woman was about to faint from anxiety, Paul's father gently took her arms and led her inside, seating her in a chair in the hall.

"Hush," he said soothingly. "Tell me, why are you so worried?"

Trembling, Dona Jiménez answered, "They left early today, to join Rodrigo, even though Don Pedro and I are continually forbidding them–"

"Just a moment," Don Carreras interrupted

He helped her lean back against the wall, slipping a cushion behind her shoulders. Paul remained where he was, his chest still heaving with exertion, and he glanced from the weak Dona Maria, his godmother, to the doorway where his brother had disappeared.

Diego had been inside the home many times before and knew his way to the kitchen well. Pushing open the carved wooden door, he stepped inside, startling a girl not much younger than he.

"Diego!" she gasped, and dropping the pan she held, flung herself into the youth's arms.

"Teresa?" The youth saw the tearstains on the girl's cheeks and tried to comfort her. "You're frightened, too, aren't you?"

"My brothers never treated me roughly before," Teresa whispered. Realizing what she had done, she blushed and pulled away with a hasty apology.

"Sweet Teresa! I'm the one who's sorry for you. There's nothing wrong with what you did," Diego said kindly. "Now, your mother is still feeling ill, and my father sent me to fetch water."

The maiden swiftly fetched a glassful and followed him out to the hall, where Dona Jiménez was slowly reviving. With infinite tenderness, Teresa took the glass from Diego and bent over her mother, lovingly holding the cup to her lips. Her mother drank it gratefully, while the three men watched with softened expressions. Mother and daughter shared the same golden-brown hair, the same sweet eyes, and the same delicateness which made others so kind and protective towards them.

"Dona Maria," Paul's father said gently, "are you able to finish your story?" She nodded, and smiled gratefully at her daughter, who retreated a distance and watched from the doorway.

"After my boys returned, they were rude – even to Teresa! – and said something about Paul, and going to meet Rodrigo again. They left soon after, but I am terribly worried – this mood they are in – they have never been like that to us, and they never mention Rodrigo! I am afraid they will do something terrible!"

"How long ago did the boys leave?" Don Carreras asked quietly.

"A half-hour ago."

"Do you know what direction?"

"They were headed west, towards Horta de Santa Maria," Teresa said quietly from the doorway. Diego glanced at her and saw how pale she was. Paul stepped anxiously towards his father.

"There are three roads leading that way – we shall have to split up. Can we hurry?" His father, who had a way of calmly and quickly getting things done, nodded and bowed to the lady.

"By your leave, Dona Maria. Please rest, and try not to worry. We will take care of your sons. Teresa, stay with your mother, dear."

"Yes, sir," Teresa whispered. Don Carreras led Paul outside. Diego lingered a moment, glancing back at Teresa, who stepped after him, trembling, her hands clasped, looking as if she was having an emotional battle.

"Diego," she pleaded, "Please – I love my brothers, and they *are* good to me – please help them!"

"Teresa . . ." Diego stooped, taking her hands, and looked tenderly into her eyes. "Don't worry. My father will do all he can for them. What they have already done is wrong, and they must be taken to task. I can promise you that we will be no harder on them than we must."

He kissed her hand and dashed after his father and brother. The three swung on their horses and galloped towards Horta de Santa Maria, but plunged to a halt when the road forked.

"Diego, you take this road," his father bade him. "Paul and I will take the other."

"As you wish!" Diego wheeled his mare and took the road on the left while his father and brother raced down the other.

After a half-mile it split again. The pair separated, with Paul taking the path on the left, and his father, the one on the right.

The sky was almost pitch black, with a lovely hint of velvety blue, but only a scattering of stars could be seen, as nearly invisible clouds covered them over. The only sound breaking the stillness of the night air over the deserted plains was the staccato beat of the horse's hooves and the whistling of the chilly air in Paul's ears.

Paul thought of all that Rodrigo had been to him throughout the years. His story was a tragic one. His only remaining family was his mother, and circumstances had separated them. Señora de Vaca worked in a dressmaking shop. Her days were long, and she spent much of the night sewing by candlelight. Her employment had separated her from her son fifteen years ago, shortly after her husband had died, having contracted a deadly illness when working on a high rooftop on a bitterly cold and snowy December day. Rodrigo had been just five years of age.

Leaving her boy in the village orphanage run by the Dominican nuns had caused Señora de Vaca not a little pain, though it mingled with the joy of his prospective religious education, which was better than what she could give. Rodrigo, however, had quickly grown bitter about his father's death and the loss of his mother's presence.

He had taken to bullying other children at the orphanage, instead of being sympathetic and kind; deceiving the sweet-tempered nuns, instead of being honest, obedient and respectful; and to stealing things, instead of growing generous and diligent. Yet there had been a time when Rodrigo loved God above all people and pleasures and goods; and he never, not even once in his life, denied the Mother of God of his love and respect. Perhaps because she had become the only mother figure left visible to him.

As for his relationship with Paul, they had been friends in the days of the orphanage; Rodrigo had intervened when another youngster was making trouble for Paul in the street, and from then on, they were as brothers. But as Rodrigo grew older, his love of mischief had become the only driving passion in his life, as though he were taking his pain out of himself and putting it back into the world.

Their twinned escapades had started young, and been kept a secret for some time, until they had been caught cutting the convent bell ropes after locking the good priest in the sacristy. Punishments and warnings had availed neither. Yet Rodrigo had always been there to pull Paul out of scrapes, put him in a good mood, and yes, teach him his ways, though he hadn't meant ill.

Paul saw those errors now. As Iria had served to draw the poison from him, he could only hope to do the same for Rodrigo in payment. *Ave Maria, gratia plena. . .*

The road seemed to stretch on and on, and Paul, chilled almost to the bone by now, couldn't help wondering how long he could stay in the saddle. How could his mount bear such a gallop at such a temperature? It was as if someone had just dunked him into a crystal-clear melting winter spring, and Paul shivered. He imagined he saw a little blaze of gold flickering beside a rock a distance off the road ahead.

"How warm that color is," he thought, shivering again. Then he realized that it was a campfire, and instinctively drew back on the reins. His horse whinnied softly, wondering why they were stopping in the middle of such a glorious run. Paul took no notice, peering intently at the fire.

Straining his eyes, he could just barely make out three figures and their mounts, shadowed by the flickering flames. One of them had a very familiar arrogant slouch. Paul dismounted, half-angry, half-troubled.

Here goes my promise to Iria, out the window, he thought. He couldn't go back to let his father and Diego know, nor could he successfully bring back all three. There was a chance he could get Alexandre and Francisco to cooperate, but he doubted Rodrigo would be willing to listen for more than thirty seconds. He ground-tied his steed. With a parting pat on the neck, he left the impatient stallion standing by the road among the brush.

The three men were sitting and standing about the fire. All was silence, as Rodrigo whittled a random branch and Alexandre stared off into the night with angry eyes. Only Francisco did not have his back to Paul. He, however, was staring down at the fire, deep in thought.

"Good evening." Paul melted out of the shadows with no warning and stood half-masked between the flickering flames and the night sky. He gave Alexandre and Francisco a shock.

"Oh," Alexandre said uneasily. "It's you."

The wind whispered through the tall grasses in response. Rodrigo cast a languid glance upwards. Flakes of wood fell from his knife and crackled at the foot of the fire.

"So," he murmured, eyes sparking. "Tell me about the bonfire."

"The rain dampened its spirits. We only barely rescued the child trapped inside. No thanks to you, verily."

The chill that settled over the Jiménez boys dimmed the fire as their eyes slid to Rodrigo. The flying shards of wood faltered, and the knife jammed in the branch, but only for a moment. "Good enough. But you didn't come here just to tell me that, did you."

"Come back to Santa Carina. Whatever you've done, whatever you're planning to do, don't do it. You know you'll regret it! After what you did in the leper camp. . . we're already looking for you, as you can see. I know I can't bring all three of you back with me if you choose to fight, so I ask you to come back now before you risk spending your lives in regret!" Paul urged.

"Rodrigo, I think we should, especially with that little girl–" Francisco began, but Rodrigo cut him off.

"Whiteliver! That snake bite years ago must have drained your courage and replaced it with its poison," he snapped.

"That's no way to treat my brother!" Alexandre said furiously.

"On the contrary, I think Francisco is the brave one," Paul interjected quietly. "And because of it, all will be easier for him when he returns than for you. My father has much in store for you, Rodrigo."

"I'm very afraid!" Rodrigo spat, laughing. He stood before Paul, his face threateningly close. "No one," he whispered, "gets to design my life but me. My parents were forced to destroy my life and leave me to building it alone. Stay out of my way, Paul."

"I almost wish I could, 'Rigo," Paul sighed. "I have to try and stop you."

"From looting an overly gilded church? Yes, you should." Rodrigo turned away and grabbed the saddlebags he had briefly laid aside from his steed. "Stop me, Paul." There was a bitter angry glow cast over his face that could have been from the campfire if his hand had not already been clenched to strike.

Paul's eyes went to the Jiménez boys, but they seemed too uneasy to move. "Try to get away, then," he said resignedly. Rodrigo reached to gather the reins.

"In that case. . . you can take it!" He whirled and struck at Paul's already swollen jaw. But Paul was as quick as he, and he ducked not a moment too soon, only to have his legs swept out from under him. Rodrigo pounced as Paul barely rolled away from the flames.

It was a difficult match for either of them to take. Don Carreras had trained Paul well, but Rodrigo had trained him, too.

The other boys stood by, staring anxiously. Why they couldn't make up their minds was anyone's guess, including their own.

Paul flung Rodrigo back down under him and locked the youth's arms in one of his, keeping himself from getting punched in the nose by a mere hair's breadth.

"Give up, Rodrigo!" he growled. "I don't want to be your enemy!"

"Then don't be," Rodrigo snarled, and bashed his head backwards into Paul's throat. Paul choked and tumbled to the side, trying to recover the breath that he had lost. In a fight so evenly matched, a moment lost was the match lost. In his moment of swirling nausea, something cracked down on his head and everything went black.

~

Paul stirred. Everything was dark, and a ripple of pain in his head made him shudder. There was a warm sting on the back of his head. He touched it involuntarily and groaned. He opened his eyes. Everything was dim and blurred. His vision swirled and he tried to get up. Someone forced him down, but not out of concern.

"Alex, where's the rope?" Rodrigo's voice demanded.

"Here," the other muttered.

Paul's eyes flew open and he struggled, but with his aching head it was no use. Rodrigo shoved him up against the side of the old, broken wagon from which they had gathered firewood. Alexandre laced the rope around Paul's wrists and chest and through the spokes of the wheel.

The look on Paul's face must have said volumes, for Alexandre winced as he secured the rope.

"Tie it well," Rodrigo commanded. "We don't want him following us."

"You mean, *you* don't want him following *you*," Francisco snapped. He had swung his bag over his shoulder and was mounting his mare. "I might not be able to stop either of you – no, I'm not as strong as you! But I don't have to be a party to you, either!" His eyes briefly met Paul's, half in apology, half reassuringly, and before Rodrigo could grab the horse's bridle, Francisco kicked her into a gallop. The hoofbeats faded into the night as Rodrigo stared, fists clenched in frustration. He whirled.

"Get a move on, Alex," he snarled. "With your brother off to who-knows-where, I'm sure we have far less safety than we thought."

The eldest Jiménez glanced up. He studied Rodrigo for a moment and then dropped his head and nodded. Rodrigo kicked sand over the fire. Alexandre gave the rope a last tug.

"Knowing you, you'll be able to get out of this in just an hour or two," he whispered. "We'll be back by then, I think— I'll try to get him to come back, anyway. If he doesn't, he's planning on heading through the Valley of the Angel's Fall!"

Paul nodded almost imperceptibly, head pounding. His eyes watched as Rodrigo saluted him, half-mockingly, and both men rode out of the camp. His vision dimmed again as the blood pounded in his temples. But he had to try and free himself – he began to work his bonds.

X

Inundation

It was cold and clear when he awoke an hour before dawn. He was cramped. The cold bit his skin but healed his headache better than ice. He moved his numbed fingers and tugged at the rope. He had loosened it considerably, enough to break loose at a moment's notice if Rodrigo returned. He rested his head back against the wheel. Only a few stars lit the velvety sky now, and his gray eyes picked out Sirius from amongst the rest. A soft whinny, followed by an answering nicker told Paul where he was.

The boulder would have been a dead giveaway in sunlight, but at night, it was hard to tell that he was in the farthest stretch of the property belonging to a family friend. Santiago was his name, and he raised the finest horses in Spain. His palominos had won many prizes, and many of the stallions and mares bore heroic knights in battle.

A strange pounding sound came to his attention. It sounded like someone was riding fast, the hoofbeats muffled by the still, foggy air. Maybe it was his father. Or Diego. Then he could get out of here and go home. More likely it was Rodrigo and Alexandre. The latter proved to be correct.

The pair brought their horses to a rearing halt a distance away, near the palominos' pasture. They were arguing. Rodrigo dismounted, saddlebags in hand, and slapped his mare's hindquarters, sending her back in the direction from whence they had come. Alexandre dismounted too, gesturing towards Paul.

"If you dare go near him, I'll make you regret it!" Rodrigo raised his voice. The wind carried his words to Paul's ears. "If they track our horses, they'll find him and think he did it, and that's just fine with me! Now, get out of here if you want to!"

Alexandre gave him a furious look, glanced at Paul, and wheeled his horse about. He soon disappeared in the direction that Francisco had taken, toward home. Rodrigo shook his head and vaulted the fence. A new mount without shoes would offer him a better chance of not being followed.

"Yah!" he cried, and leapt onto the back of a gentle filly. She leapt the fence at his bidding.

Paul tore himself free of the ropes, knowing he couldn't let Rodrigo get out of sight. It would be easy to lose him in the canyons for which he was headed. He gave a sharp whistle, praying that Rafael had remained nearby.

Answering hoofbeats brought relief, and a rush of wind in his ears as he swung on. The ground whirled away beneath Rafael's hooves as they chased the faint glimmer of gold in the distance, nearly lost in the gray of dawn, that was Rodrigo's filly.

Emerald foothills morphed into towering, rocky slopes, which plunged away with heart-wrenching suddenness into a widening river gorge, roughly cut as though the river had spent centuries trying to hew it as a diamond. Iron shoes clattered on stone of rust and ashen hue as Rodrigo rode in the shallows and Paul on the bank, one to hide and one to lead.

The river ran jade green and silver waterfalls misted over the gray outcroppings. Then there was a crack of thunder. A bright white bolt split the sky, and Rodrigo's filly whinnied in fright.

A rainstorm had come out of nowhere, masked by the violet sky. Drops poured down with the velocity of hail, pelting Paul's unprotected head, and the impact on the river sounded like the shattering of glass. The ominous rolls of thunder warned Paul that the storm would not stop quickly enough.

His hair drenched, water dripped into his eyes, making it even more impossible to make out *anything* through the solid sheet of rain before his face. Rafael wasn't happy either, nicking his hooves on stones in the path, as blind as he.

"Rodrigo!" Paul yelled. Somehow his voice came echoing back at him. A sudden remembering fear was clenching his heart. Not a mile up the gorge from where they stood was an ancient dam, a remnant from Roman days. It had threatened to burst the previous summer, with the record rainfall. Now, he could see the river groaning with the weight of melted snow, combined with the flash of rain the day before, and the storm now. There was no time.

"Rodrigo!" he yelled again, straining his vocal cords. "We need to get out of the gorge! The dam will break!"

Rodrigo only heard the half of it, but his scoffing voice came back at his follower, not a furlong behind.

"It's held this long, what makes you think a little rain is going to hurt it? Get on, Paul!" The rain softened, just for an instant, and Rodrigo reined in the filly by the mane, hearing hoofbeats approaching rapidly from somewhere to the right. But it wasn't Paul; turning around, through the briefly lightened rain he could see that Paul, too, had stopped.

Rodrigo sent his mount bolting. The hoofbeats herded him up the riverside. A rider at such a pace in this weather could very well be someone who knew what he had done, and the treasures he carried with him. His eyes were set on a steep ramp worn into the side of the gorge by hooves and weather. Never mind that it was dangerously slippery in the rain.

"Get out of the ravine, Paul, if you're afraid of the water!" he yelled over his shoulder.

Paul frowned and nudged Rafael after him. "Come on!" he breathed.

"Paul?" a voice suddenly came calling through the rain, halfway across the river. Rafael snorted at the sharpness with which Paul jerked the reins.

"Iria?!" His heart was beating in his ears. Looking down over the side of the precipice he could make out a figure dismounted on a narrow spit of sand that jutted out through the water. Fernando's horse was on the bank. Somehow, Iria had known where to find them. Somehow, she had known to come directly southwest and cut through the hills.

"Iria! Get out of the gorge!" he screamed at her. "Go back!"

"No! He called me here, Paul, and He doesn't want me to—"

"Iria! The rain is flooding the—"

His warning was cut off by a massive creaking crash and groan from up the canyon. Terrified, Fernando's horse fled, jerking the reins from Iria's hand as she tried to pull him back.

"Iria, RUN!" Paul cried desperately, kicking his heels into Rafael's side and trying to turn him around on the narrow ledge that held them back. If he could get down there, he could grab her—

Rodrigo had turned at the screams, already standing precariously high on the gorge's rim. A wave of horror chilled every blood cell in his veins as a thundering wall of mud and water swept through the valley, inundating the already swollen river. Everything that lay in the gorge was drowned with it.

"IRIA!" Paul's scream cut the air even through the rolling thunder. He kicked free of the stirrups and was gone, disappearing in the roaring torrent. As the earthquake steadied to a drumroll and the river fell, not a trace appeared of man or maiden.

The wind wrapped its cold arms around Rodrigo, alone on the clifftop. His wet skin froze with the same alacrity as his heart. Over the storm, no one could hear the bells pealing for Palm Sunday. He had killed them both.

XI

Ramification

A stroke of velvet found Rodrigo's chilled fingers. The youth unknowingly stroked Rafael's muzzle. He had led the stallion and the filly across the muddy hills until a mountain glade had opened before them, hanging on the fringe of a nobleman's distant orchard. Here he sought refuge. The trees grew almost wild and dripped with moss, and the buds of lemon mingled with the red of a few late apples. The grass ran ragged among the stones and an outcropping of rock ran with melted snow.

Rodrigo dropped Rafael's reins. The stallion had had no place to go, save upwards, when his master had vaulted from the saddle. He was loyal enough to have followed if horse sense had deemed it doable. But the filly had needed a strong shoulder after her fright, and this sodden human seemed to need one, too.

Rodrigo was not an unfamiliar nor unwelcome sight to his eyes by any means; he somehow knew there was something not quite right with the man's character, but being a horse, it wasn't an issue for him. Except that he had seen Rodrigo strike Paul, and that was not something to be allowed. But then there was still the filly, and something wrong with Rodrigo. So, Rafael had been the one to truly lead. Rodrigo could scarcely have seen the ground before his feet.

Rafael's ears flicked backwards as he looked at the youth, perhaps briefly wondering if he ought to return the strike with a good bite on the sleeve. But they swiveled again as Rodrigo sank to the grass and dropped his head in his hands. No, the human was too tired to be bitten, he judged. He turned to the filly instead.

She had caught a chill in the rain and stood shivering under a lemon tree. Rafael gently bumped her nose with his. There was no sense in being distracted while she was freezing. He lay down, his back against the tree, and let her lean on him to keep warm. He only wished his master were there to take them all home.

Rodrigo gazed into the void of shadow that filled his eyelids. His heart felt tight in his chest. No, he had not struck man or maiden down with his hands. The flood had done that. But it was his roguery that had led them there at the time of the flood. Why hadn't the flood swept him away instead? Why couldn't he have been going down into the ravine with them behind, and not up?

His dead brown eyes watched restlessly as he played with Paul, so many years ago, in his memory. Someone had tried to come between them once. Drama had ensued, with many varied escapades and finally they had gotten around the offender. For a time, each had been made to think that the other had rejected their fellow prankster.

When they had reassured themselves that it was not so, Paul had grasped his adopted brother's hands and said, *We'll always be friends, won't we, 'Rigo? Even if circumstances make it seem otherwise?*

Of course, little brother, Rodrigo had said, and meant it.

Oh, the fool! The idiocy! His bitter revenge on the world had dealt revenge upon himself. In his feelings of betrayal, he had thereby killed his best friend. No man could survive that torrent of silt and raging water. And there was no chance in heaven that the girl could have.

He was an outcast now, he thought. With no place to lay his head, he could do as he pleased, take what he pleased – he could roam all of Spain and no one would find him. But this was the sort of thinking that had brought him into this catastrophe.

Rodrigo bit his lip until it bled. The outcast life was the only way to go. It fit what he had always done. But he couldn't - he couldn't risk further consequences – but he had destroyed his life. The road back had been washed away in the flood.

"Little son," a voice spoke softly. Rodrigo's eyes snapped open. He had been so lost that he hadn't heard footfalls upon the wet grass. A young woman, whose head could scarcely have come to his shoulder, knelt before him, looking into his eyes. Her hair and eyes were dark and her skin deeply tanned from the sun. Her clothing was worn from years of wear, the deep blue of her dress blackened near the hem and faded over the shoulders. Her mantle was worn ivory and yellow and a young child peeked out from behind her skirts.

"Little son," she repeated, "are you well?"

"I – no – I'm just resting on my journey," Rodrigo answered lamely, trying to regain his composure. He tried to place what was so familiar about her face.

"Ah," the woman murmured. "As are we." She drew her son into her lap and gently kissed his golden curls. "Don Esteban has removed us from his lands." She looked up at the trees that waved overhead, patching over the now golden-gray sky. "This orchard was ours to tend, once. But slowly he took our lives away, and now the orchard with it. We must leave, ere we perish. If only there were someplace to welcome us, but I fear empty hearts grow more commonplace than these lemons."

Rodrigo looked into the rosy face of the child, almost asleep on his mother's shoulder. It was true, that both, while beautiful, were also fading. He squared his shoulders and arose. His limbs were strong, and swinging into the apple tree above him was far easier than scaling the abbey wall. He plucked two red-cheeked apples and dropped down beside the pair once more.

"Here," he said, holding the fruits out to them. "Your lives were not his to take. I assure you that you will find what you need in Santa Carina. There is a convent there where you

might find refuge and work; if not, go to the Carreras villa—
I'm sure they would not turn you away." He took Rafael's reins
and gently pulled the stallion from the filly's side. "This horse
belongs to them. . . his master left him with me. They will
appreciate it if you return him."

"My little son," the woman said with a soft smile, and
leaning from the saddle, gently brushed back the waves from
his forehead. Her child looked at him with gray eyes that
were far too deep for such a young one, and the look grew
hard and then soft once more.

"Thou thief," he said, in a voice so clear Rodrigo jumped
and stared back. "Wilt thou steal heaven as you have stolen
these apples? Soon will I see thee open the gates."

"We will see you anon, Rodrigo," the woman murmured,
and her eyes were glowing with her smile. She clucked softly
to Rafael. The stallion didn't hesitate to pick his way through
the trees and gallop across the fields.

Rodrigo stood, feet frozen to the mud, as the speck of
black and blue and white faded amongst the green below. He
knew now that face. With a numb hand, he slipped his hand
into the saddlebag still slung over his shoulder. Amongst the
jeweled and golden flowers pried from the wall of ex votos,
he found the painting of a woman and her son. The Woman.
. .. the Child.

Drumming hoofbeats drew upon his ears and the filly
whinnied. But it was Diego who dismounted. His green-gray
eyes knew the truth.

"It's time to go home, Rodrigo." His voice was quiet enough to have been uttered in the convent walls.

A rope was slipped around his hands, but Rodrigo didn't resist. There was nowhere left for him to run. . . not anymore.

~

Paul stirred. A rising pain crept through his head, chest and spine. He tried to remember why and wondered why it was so dark. Gradually the memory of mud against his face and the roar of water came back to him. The last thing he had known was a hand feeling for his pulse, and the murmur of Fernando's voice and his father's, saying that they would take him home.

After that. . . everything had gone dark again, save for the occasional swirl of voices at his bedside. It was Marina's that he had mostly heard, singing softly and speaking to him as she had done her best to heal him. It didn't seem that anyone was with him now.

Paul struggled to open his eyes but found a weight upon them. He realized that the pressure was that of a wet cloth. The youth reached upwards to remove it but a numbing pain shot through his arm and he wisely chose to desist.

What was it that had happened? Paul thought again of the sound of rushing water and felt his pulse leap far too high. The flood! Yes, it was the flood. And Rodrigo – and–

"Iria!" Paul's voice broke the silence. His spine screamed in protest as he snapped upright amongst the cushions, and the cloth fell from his eyes. His room was dark, too dark. The thought came of Imelda and her own darkened room. He groaned. Had both perished? The rustling of skirts and hastening footsteps drew his eyes to the door.

"Mother?"

"Paul, my precious," Dona Rosita whispered, coming and sitting beside him. She laid her cool hand on his brow. "You should stay lying down. You aren't healed yet, though Marina has done her best for you. It's a miracle that the flood washed you up onto the bank."

"Mother–" Paul's frightened eyes investigated her mirrored ones. The question couldn't force itself to his lips. Dona Rosita knew what he was asking.

"Imelda is well, dear," she smiled reassuringly. "Your father told me of your pilgrimage. I think that did much good."

A shaky breath escaped Paul. That left only one life to worry about. "And – Iria?" he whispered anxiously. "I couldn't find her – I tried to get to her but I couldn't–"

An expression of distress flashed over his mother's face. "They're . . . still searching for her, Paul. Offer up your pain for her, please, dear."

"How long," he asked haggardly.

". . . Three days."

Her son sucked his breath in so sharply it hurt. Images of Iria, buried beneath feet of mud and silt, caught upon some boulder in the river, or floating unseen by night crowded his mind.

"If they found me, they can still find her," he said, praying that it was true.

Another footstep was heard in the hall. "Paul?" It was Fernando. He came and looked down at the injured boy.

"Why did you let her go?" Paul growled.

Fernando bit his lip. It was clear that he hadn't slept for some time and his eyes were worn by tears. "We didn't," he said. "She was so exhausted when you left. . . I thought she'd die that night. We left her to rest during the evening meal but when we returned, she was missing. . .and so was Ora. She must have ridden him all the way. . . but. . . he didn't get caught in the flood. He came home with Rafael. I still haven't sent the news to my family. I still hope not to have the need. . . ."

Paul closed his eyes again, feeling the pain and the fear pounding through his body. If the Virgin had saved Imelda from the brink of death – saved him from his past – brought him out of the flood – it wasn't too late for Iria to be found. Alive.

All he could do was hope, but he feared that it was not the hope he was meant to have. If – and his mind could scarcely allow the thought – if she was in heaven now, with the only One who could love her as she deserved, his heart was drawn to be where hers was and to find her in God. Living would be like a long, sorrowful dream until the rainbow broke once more.

"All we can do is keep searching," he said. His gray eyes turned towards the shuttered window. It was going to be a long day.

~

The past three days had dragged on for Rodrigo. He had been in a daze and half frozen when Diego had brought him in. Don Carreras, despite his misgivings, had pitied him. There was an ancient cell in the wine cellar where the boys had played years ago; he put it to its old use and let Rodrigo remain there, better cared for than in the town prison.

The treasures Rodrigo had stolen had been returned to the chapel of Our Lady of Estrella by the Padre. The priest there, having heard the tale, agreed not to tell anyone of it. Rodrigo was left supposedly innocent as far as anyone outside of the family was concerned. For this he was grateful. He was relieved, too, when he heard that Paul had not perished.

The youth was left on his own on the bench in his cell, from which he had a view of the wine stores and flickering candlelight. Now and then the gray cat, Fresa, would rub up against the bars and purr before departing to hunt for mice. He could hear her pounce, her nails clacking on the wooden barrels.

No one came to visit him save the servant who would bring food. But even his appearance became infrequent, for Rodrigo wouldn't touch anything, much less eat it. It wasn't from the stomachache, which might have been from the chill he had caught. It might have been the pain in his heart. Every time he closed his eyes, he found more.

His eyes flew open when he heard light footsteps descending the stairs, faltering at the last. They weren't those of the servant, whose heavy steps made the cellar ring. It was Marina who was silhouetted in the entry, and she came and stood before him. He arose and faced her sullen gaze.

"I know you didn't mean for harm to come to anyone," she said at last, quietly. The candlelight danced over her dark hair and illuminated her deep eyes.

"No," Rodrigo whispered, turning his head away from her. "I didn't know about the child in the chapel. . . and why couldn't I have been going down, and not up? Why did he have to follow me?"

Marina could see the tear sparkling on his cheek even in the shadows. "It's never easy to know the consequences. It wasn't truly your fault. . . the flood wasn't of your doing. He's going to be alright. It's never too late for you to just let God love you," she said gently.

Rodrigo's expression eased. "It isn't?"

Marina shook her head.

The boy took a deep breath and turned back to her. "I wish they'd find the girl. I don't want your brother to hate me."

"He won't hate you," Marina murmured. She studied his face. "I'm not really supposed to be down here," she admitted. "I begged my father to let me talk to you since you're ill. We used to be close friends, once."

Rodrigo gave a wry smile. "That was before I did the things that I did, and your father couldn't let you have such a one for a friend. He's right, you know. It's not proper for a gentle one to speak to me now."

"No," she agreed, and hesitated. "But you won't be doing such things anymore," she stated, lifting her chin.

"No," he echoed. "I won't."

A smile crossed her face. "Then we can be friends again, Ro."

Rodrigo found himself smiling, too, and the pain lessened. "You haven't called me that since you were a baby. I used to call you Daisy, didn't I."

"I know," she said. "I've missed you." She glanced down for a moment. "I'll ask my father if I may take care of you. Now, promise me you'll eat what I bring you?"

"Promise." Rodrigo rested his cheek on the bars as Marina disappeared up the stairs.

~

The fourth and fifth day passed. There was no sign of Iria. Paul could see by his parents' eyes, and even Fernando's, that they had lost hope. A shudder ran through his soul that threatened to tear him in twain.

All was quiet and dim in the room as everyone left him alone. Dust slowly floated about the room, illuminated by the shafts of sunlight. Faintly, Paul heard the bells tolling, and wondered how it was that they weren't as silent as he. He closed his eyes. His head ached. He remained in bed that day, and the next.

Finally, Paul begged his mother to let him up. She helped him walk about until she was sure that he would be alright on his own. Paul slowly moved about the house. His heart was heavy and dull with pain.

He hardly saw the sunlight dancing over the floor as it streamed through the windows; he hardly heard the joyous song of the birds. The sky was not a glorious blue, but gray as a warning for him; the clouds were not soft and picturesque, but heavy with sorrow and late pain; to him, it was not the falling of burning, autumn leaves, but the afternotes of death.

It was not the emerald grass he saw, but the hush of icy snow in winter; not the kind that was soft, beautiful, and the makings of an innocent new world, but the freezing, crushing paleness of suffocating death. He could no longer see the roses that bloomed, nor the sparkling brook that crossed the lawn; all he saw was dreariness, and darkness, and bleakness, and sorrow.

Paul leaned heavily against the frame of the window and looked out bleakly at his old world. His thoughts were silenced. His heart was silenced.

"Behold, I long for Thee, O Lord: bid me come!" And he laid his head upon the glass.

XII

Passion

It was a soft, sad voice that wakened Paul from his dreamless, waking sleep.

"Angel?" It was Imelda. She stood uncertainly before him, her eyes wide with sorrowful concern. Paul slowly drew himself up from where he leaned upon the window frame. It was the first time he had seen her since she had left for the convent. A smile tugged on his lips despite the pain and he put his arms around her.

"Yes, sweet." His voice was as hushed as hers. She laid her little hands uncertainly upon his knee.

"Is Angel well?" A sad smile was the only answer he could give her. The little child sighed and laid her head on his knee. Her curls were stroked gently in response; at least he was no longer in a trance.

"Mommy's looking for you, Angel," the little one whispered.

Paul gently lifted her and put her head on his shoulder. He stepped through the house. He found his mother in the kitchen with Marina and Diego. All were dressed in shades of black and blue. It was then that Paul realized it was Good

Friday. The bells he had heard had marked the death of Christ.

Marina hastened to slip her arms about his neck and gently kiss his cheek. "Are you well?"

Paul could give no answer save to wind one of her curls around his fingers. Dona Rosita gently laid her hand on his shoulder.

Diego, putting down his glass, came and gently hugged his brother. "It's good to see you on your feet, little brother. You'll want news, I think. . . Alexandre and Francisco told us everything when they came back that night, and are presently merely grounded. The stolen goods were returned and Rodrigo, well, he's in the cellar. I think he could use a visit from you."

Paul nodded listlessly, muttered a thank you, and soon found himself in his old haunt. For once, he wasn't there to steal wine. Rodrigo was slumped on the bench, lost in thought. His fever had lessened with Marina's care and the food she had made for him.

"Paul!" He looked up as his friend entered. "I'm glad that they found you." He spoke hesitantly, unsure of how Paul was feeling towards him.

"Yes," Paul said quietly. He was limping a bit. Marina had healed him well, but his back still jarred with every step. His mind was locked in prayer and the thought of Iria.

"No news?"

Paul shook his head.

"Why? Why did you two have to follow me?" Rodrigo moaned.

"It wasn't directly your fault, Rodrigo. You didn't – kill – us."

"No, the flood nearly did," Rodrigo said bitterly. "It's my fault for going there."

"Did you hear what she said in the gorge?" Paul asked slowly.

"No."

"She said God called her there. Even if you hadn't been there. . . you don't know. She might have been there still. Face it, Rodrigo. If she hadn't come, you would have been in the gorge. You wouldn't have gone up. . . you would have drowned."

Rodrigo froze as it sank in. "She saved my life." He slammed his fists on the stone wall of the cellar. "Why, why?" he gasped again.

"'Rigo. . . we would have lost you. I don't regret that you're still here."

"The fact that it's not entirely my fault doesn't help," Rodrigo muttered. "I'm not going to be able to live with my-self now."

Paul's eyes narrowed with what was almost a bitter smile. "Then let's go look for her. I need to know. . . I need to find her . . . even if she isn't. . ."

Rodrigo stared at him. "I know you're not allowed to leave the house in your condition."

"We-ell–"

"Paul, I thought I lost you once, little brother. I'm not going to risk your injury again, and I'm not about to make people think I'm trying to escape."

"Rodrigo, please! One last time." Paul's eyes were desperate.

Rodrigo sighed but the old smirk tugged on his lips. "One last time," he agreed.

Paul drew the keys he had borrowed and released his friend from the cell. "We'll go saddle the horses. I don't know where your mare is now, so you can borrow one of ours."

They took the stairs two at a time and hastened up the hall. Both collided with Fernando, who was returning from Marina's care for his fatigue.

He blinked, wondering whether he was fully awake. "Where are you two going, might I ask?"

Paul coughed. "To look for your sister." He tried to sidle past but Fernando blocked him with one arm.

"You know you're not supposed to leave the house, both of you. *He's* not even supposed to leave the cellar."

"I can't stay here any longer," Paul said quietly. "I'll go crazy far more quickly than I'll reinjure my spine, I can assure you that. Please let us go, Fernando."

Fernando shook his head slowly. "I guess that makes three of us then. I'm not supposed to leave either, but I can't take it."

No sooner had they opened the front door than they faced Diego. He surveyed the three. "We're going hunting," said Paul. "Please, De! I need closure. I need – her."

"How many times have I told you not to call me that," Diego said with a small smile.

"I was hoping that if I annoy you, you'll let us go."

"Hardly," he replied. "But since I can't stop all three of you, I'll have to go along with you this time." He herded them to the stables.

~

The mud sucked at the horses' hooves as they picked their way along the riverbank. The river Llorando had flooded to twice its size and only now were the waters beginning to retreat, leaving silt and quartz stones covering the valley floor.

Paul eyed the smooth green and turquoise band that moved like liquid glass, seemingly so guiltless and docile now. He could see Fernando and Francisco combing the opposite bank. Rodrigo, Alexandre, and Diego were occupying the same bank as he.

Diego had the responsibility of keeping an eye on every one of the miscreants and wondered why he hadn't made a job of babysitting. The Jiménez boys had joined the search despite being grounded. Don Pedro had let them go only at Paul's behest.

Six troubled hearts pounded alongside the placid river, each one with its own visions of fear. A lifeless body, or a lifeless river. No one wanted to admit that they had little to no hope left. A week had gone by. Unless some stranger had rescued her and said nothing, there was not likely much to find. The sun was arching lower and lower overhead; it would be evening soon.

Paul heard a frustrated exclamation from Rodrigo. "Ay, she could have floated down to the sea by now!" he growled. "What on earth am I doing, combing a river not an hour's float from the flood when she's been missing a week?"

"I know the feeling," Paul muttered. "We'll keep moving. We won't give up, Rodrigo, not I leastways, until we reach the sea."

If she had floated so far – anyone could have fished her out: peasants, knights, and pagans alike. Paul tried not to stab his tongue with his teeth in payment for that dose of mental pain. There was nothing but bits of wood and torn up vegetation beneath Rafael's hooves. The stallion did not appreciate the mud that seemed to squelch endlessly onwards.

Paul took pity on him and pulled him up onto a flat rock that gave him a slightly better view of the area. He scanned both sides of the river. He hadn't expected to see anything, yet his heart still sank. There were no signs along the bank that pointed in Iria's direction. His eyes instead fell upon a small island in the river. Normally it was in the center, but with the flooding it was closer to the west bank. He could see a flurry of trees tangled with jacaranda blossoms and rushes.

"Ah, yes, that island." Alexandre had come up beside him. "They've started saying it's haunted. Doesn't look it, with those blossoms."

"Haunted?" Paul repeated. "Since when?"

"Since–" Alexandre broke off with a strange look. "Since the flood."

"De!" Paul almost shouted.

"Paul, truly? I asked you to stop calling me that," Diego said patiently, joining them.

"The island. Has it been searched?"

Diego stared at his brother's wild eyes. "The water's been too high!"

Paul whirled his mount, and they plunged into the icy Llorando. Rodrigo, Alexandre, and Diego didn't hesitate to follow. Their horses kicked against the current and kept their heads above the water. Their riders didn't escape a drenching, but they didn't notice. Francisco and Fernando saw them reaching the island and urged their mounts to meet them.

"Split up!" Diego commanded.

The island, at only a couple of acres in size, wouldn't have taken long to search if it hadn't been so thoroughly covered in a net of lush vines and trees. The constant flooding of the low island meant that the thin soil was richer than most, and so the plants thrived. In so doing, they busied themselves catching in the boys' hair and tearing at their cloaks and tunics, leaving each one stranded every few moments until he managed to hack away at the offending branches.

Quite a few scratches later, the verdict was pronounced. The island was as hopeless as the riverbanks. Paul's heart felt heavy in his chest as he reached for Rafael's reins. Rodrigo was right. They might as well be combing the sea.

"It seems we have company," Francisco raised his voice. Paul turned. A nobleman dressed in a rich cloak of carmine velvet and a tunic of strained ocean blue was fording the river. It was Barón Esteban Diaz, former knight. His extensive estate lay on the west bank of the river, and stretched northwards just to the fringes of Santa Carina, crossing in an arc through the mountains and valleys to encompass a number of orchards. Rodrigo growled internally.

"What's wrong?" Paul muttered.

"He threw her out," Rodrigo said resentfully.

"What? Who?"

"He threw Our Lady out."

Paul didn't get a chance to question him further.

"Pray tell, what are you doing on my island?" the Barón inquired, his steed advancing though the shallows.

"Forgive us, sir, our good sister was caught in the flood last week and hasn't been found," Diego answered, stepping forward and trying to silence the indignant men behind him. "This island is one of the few places we have not searched. Had we realized it was yours, we would have asked for your blessing."

The Barón eyed him for a moment. "Your sister, you say. A maiden with hair the deepest brown of the eagle's wings, and eyes tinted like an iris?"

Paul opened his mouth to answer, then stopped. He didn't even know what color Iria's eyes were because of the shadow that always found them from her veil. Fernando pushed him out of the way.

"Yes! Where is she?"

Barón Esteban Diaz frowned. "She's in my home, being cared for. She is not dead, as you have feared; I pulled her from the rushes not two days ago, and she has been in a deep sleep since from which none can awaken her."

Paul's heart twisted in mixed feelings of painful relief and anxiety. There was a moment in which everyone drew a sigh, trying to make it silent but failing.

"And you didn't know of the search?" Fernando asked sharply. "It would have been honorable of you to let her family know."

The Barón settled his reins with an air of annoyance. "I have been loath to give her up. She is not the kind which one can give up, very easily, as you can attest to. No harm will come to her where she is, I assure you. I will let you see her since you are her family." He turned his horse about and sloshed through the river.

"Is it just me, or would we all like to clobber him," Rodrigo growled.

"Verily," Paul and Fernando said together.

"Peace!" Diego sighed. "Despite our efforts, he saved her life more assuredly than we have." He waved them after him, and the parade began to the other side of the Llorando.

XIII

Devotion

The Barón's red brick and sandstone manor rose into the spring sky, set amongst the hills like a musical effigy. The sunlight was slanting low, giving the stones a fiery hue as the group rode into the spacious courtyard. Tropical plants, taken from conquered Moorish gardens, grew in abundance beside budding poppies, nodding in a sweet breeze that comforted Paul.

The smell of stew and baking bread mingled with the scent of roses and almond blossoms as they dismounted. They found themselves at the right side of the home, the wide staircase meandering down from the patio among vines and fronds. A limestone fountain bubbled and bounced, sending a soft mist on the breeze and kissing the nodding roses climbing on the courtyard walls.

A mourning dove cooed from up above, perched on a limb of an oak entwined by a violet wisteria vine, and several squirrels ran about, gathering acorns for the coming winter. The perfume of the wildflowers of a maiden's little flowerbed mingled with the strong scents of rosemary, basil, and lavender from the kitchen garden. The maiden whose hands tended these plots despite her nobility was seated upon the patio, bent over her embroidery.

"Amapola, my daughter!" the Barón called.

Paul froze. Amapola, looking for sweeter and more maidenly than usual, glanced up and then leapt to her feet, her work falling on the stones, scattering needles and thread, and causing the dove to abruptly stop cooing, a lizard to scurry out of the way, and several sparrows to flit about in a race to gather fresh nesting materials.

"*Ave Maria Purissima!*" she cried breathlessly. She had been taken by surprise at the number of guests, and she tamed her wild curls with a velvet ribbon that matched her ruby kirtle.

"*Sin Peccado Concepida*!" Diego answered for them all, completing the old Spanish greeting that honored the doctrine of the Immaculate Conception.

Paul's eyes were wide. 'Oooh no," he muttered. "Um, Rodrigo, you didn't happen to fix it–"

"Uh, sorry, I had a flood on my hands?"

"Rodrigoooo–" The look on Paul's face that accompanied the moan would have normally made Rodrigo laugh. He just squeezed his friend's shoulder.

"Alright, alright, I promised I'd get you out of it," he consoled Paul, as Amapola hastened down the stairs to greet her father.

"Daddy," she murmured, and he, taking her head in his hands, gently kissed her brow in greeting.

"My poppet," he said. "These men have come for our mysterious maiden. They will be spending the evening with us, as it is getting late, and will take her home in the morning. I wish you to send a messenger to their households to apprise them of this. But first, greet them, my dear."

Amapola turned obediently, golden eyes downcast as she curtsied.

"It is fair to meet you, my lady," Diego said, quite properly. He elbowed Paul and motioned for the others to say something. Alexandre and Francisco bowed and murmured something.

"How do you fare, Amapola?" Rodrigo asked easily.

She smiled at last and raised her eyes to his face. "I am well, Rodrigo, and you?"

"I think I could do better," he said, half to himself. Amapola's eyes turned at last to Paul and he winced.

". . . Good evening."

"Good evening, Paul." But she didn't seem anxious, and that confused him.

"Oh, so *you're* Paul," Barón Esteban looked him up and down. "I do wish you would have asked me before you proposed to her."

"I–" Paul spluttered, and so did Diego.

"Since when, Paul?" he demanded.

"Never!" Paul yelped.

"He was a bit intoxicated," Rodrigo interjected, quite helpfully. "He didn't realize what he said."

"Paul–" Both Diego and Barón Esteban glared at him.

"He doesn't want to marry me, Daddy!" Amapola laid her hand on his arm. "It's alright. I haven't seen him in months."

"So that's why you stopped mentioning him," the Barón understood, relaxing slightly. "A misunderstanding, then. . . quite a mix-up, which I hope has helped you to value wine a little less?"

"Most definitely," Paul mumbled, wondering what had happened.

Rodrigo grinned to himself. He had seen the way Amapola's eyes had fallen on Francisco and the answering smile in his own. It was a well-kept secret that they had been considering courtship, but Francisco had felt them both too young yet. Perhaps it explained the sudden growth of maturity in both.

Amapola led them all in to the table, spread with tureens of lentil and bean stew, cod and spinach, bread with garlic and olive oil, and deep red wines that tasted of orange and cinnamon. The aromas were inviting after a long day of fasting and hunting, though each boy frowned a little.

Normally, Good Friday for them, save Rodrigo, meant the eating of merely bread and ale or wine. This seemed too great a feast to have on the day of shared sorrow over Christ and one's sins. They would content themselves with eating as little as they could, without offending their host, but offering up the eating of it since it wasn't the fast they were accustomed to. Paul and Fernando both resisted the temptation to seat themselves and turned back to their host.

"Please, allow us to see her first."

"My aunt is tending her at the moment," Amapola said softly. Her mother's sister was a Carmelite and a skilled nurse. "Please, eat; I'm sure your sister would wish you to after such a day."

The boys reluctantly gave in and tried to bury their impatience beneath the table. There was an awkward pause when the Barón did not say grace. Amapola's eyes flickered, and she stared at her plate. Diego briefly debated whether it would be appropriate to ask permission to pray grace for them all; he didn't think so, so he motioned for everyone to pray on their own.

Rodrigo's eyebrows were drawn together, and sometime later whilst in the middle of a bite of garlic bread dipped in mushroom sauce, he nearly choked. He saw an icon cast casually in a corner as though awaiting to be thrown away.

"What's that," he asked abruptly.

The Barón followed his gaze. "Oh, an old painting to be burned. I'm redecorating, you see. I don't need that sort of thing."

"You can't throw her out!" Rodrigo's dark eyes flashed with anger. It was a look everyone in the village dreaded to face. It didn't come often, but when it did, it spelled danger.

The Barón laid down his fork, perhaps beginning to feel his peril. "May I ask why?"

"You can't throw out a woman who gave her *entire* life to save you. She gave everything in her for you. You can't erase that!" Rodrigo growled. He was blissfully unaware that his companions were in some amount of shock.

"She doesn't *need* you, and God doesn't particularly need you either, but they *choose* to need you! You don't know the consequences of turning them away. I should know. . . by choosing a similar path, I nearly caused the deaths of three people, one whom I loved and two who were innocent," he muttered. "It's my fault alone that the maid is here."

"I doubt that I could have worded that better," came a woman's voice from the top of the stairs. It was Sister Maria. She smiled, for Rodrigo had been in her charge during his time in the abbey. Her leather sandals made scarcely a sound on the steps as she came down and looked her brother-in-law squarely in the eye. "If you must remove her, give her to me; the convent is always glad of another way of honoring its Mother."

The Barón did not reply; a spot on his napkin seemed to fascinate him. "Amapola, go and return the image to your mother's room, please," he said at last. He tossed down his napkin. "Dear sister, these men have come for the maid. Please take them up at once to see her. They will take her home in the morning." He dismissed them all from the table.

"This way, please." Sister Maria ushered them up the stairs. "I'm afraid she hasn't awakened. . . I doubt if the Seven

Holy Sleepers slept any more soundly than she! But there is always hope yet."

She stopped short. A guard had been mounted outside Iria's chamber, but not on anyone's orders.

"Oh, it *would* be him," Paul muttered through gritted teeth. It was the Barón's son, Mendo, who happened to have been the 'last new friend' of Rodrigo's whom Paul had thrown out into the street.

"Mendo, move your chair aside, please. You should have been at dinner," the nun scolded.

Mendo kicked his chair back, leaning it precariously against the door as he surveyed the group. "You two, is it?" he said with a low laugh, when he saw Rodrigo and Paul. "Forgive me, Sister, but no man enters this room."

"Except you, I presume." Sister Maria's voice was flat as she grabbed his shoulder and pulled him out of the chair. "She belongs to them."

"Finders, keepers," Mendo answered airily, blocking the door once more. "She was on *our* property. It was the will of God that she be here for me to protect." His face hardened. "I won't let *anyone* touch her. I won't let anyone hurt her. Not this time."

"You – you – *flopdoodle*," Fernando snarled, struggling not to fall into a lesser vocabulary. "I'm her brother, for heaven's sake!"

"Brother or no, you didn't prove a good guardian, did you? I'm certain to take better care of her than any of *you*, who all let her be washed away! She's on our land and under our care. . . and the sweetest creature created for fourteen hundred years."

It was beginning to dawn on them all, amidst their rising anger, that the family was acting particularly peculiar and protective towards a leper. Most lived in fear and disgust of them, and even the Church tended to mark them as dead to society with a special ceremony.

"Besides," the Barón's son added with a look of spite, "*Qui tacet consentit!* I need a wife and silence gives consent, so we will wed when she awakens."

The rising growl in Fernando's throat didn't warn Mendo quickly enough. He found himself snatched by the collar of his tunic and hurled halfway down the hall. Fernando dusted off his hands.

"Brilliant," Paul said, and they lost no time pushing the chair out of the way and lifting the latch.

The late light of the sunset glowed dimly in the room, with streaks of ruby and soft gold. The river glinted in the distance through the windowpanes, the deep hue matching the curtains of the four-poster bed. There, wrapped in white and rose blankets, lay Iria.

Fernando leapt forward and bent over her. Diego had to restrain Paul. No matter his feelings for Iria, it was her brother's privilege to be the first to hold her. The others lined respectfully along the wall, Alexandre with his back against the door, lest Mendo try to interfere again.

Fernando stooped over Iria for some time in utter silence. "Paul," his voice cracked at last. "Come look." He sounded strange, almost strangled. Whether it was from pain or relief, Paul couldn't tell. Seven steps brought him to the bedside, and he felt the blood momentarily drain from his face, leaving him dizzy.

The face he saw, resting there upon the pillow amidst a glorious cloud of hair the color of polished oak, was not the face he knew. Doe-like eyes, even while shut, and deep rose-petal lips were vaguely familiar. But the shadow no longer caressed her face. Nothing was to be seen there except for a tinge of ivory. The savage sores that had torn down her face, softened by the frame of her veil, had been erased.

She lay so still. It was almost like death, not sleep. Her breath hardly creased the velvet throw laid over the covers. Not a tremor in her face gave her life away.

Fernando drew a shaky breath. His lips were trembling. "I thought for a moment that it wasn't her. Her face, Paul! Her face!" And with frightened hands he touched the skin, so cold and glassy. It couldn't have been older than a handful of sunsets, such was the softness of it against his fingertips. He pulled back the blankets a little. Iria's hands were nestled there, gloveless for the first time in over a year. Her slender fingers were markless now.

"What phantasm is this? Living death?"

Paul's heart was shivering against his ribcage, threatening to break. It was the ageless sleep that had fallen upon Iria. But she was there! The face he had thought he'd never see, never *truly* see on earth again, and yet she was silent! She was cold! Why was this pain as great as though she had not been found? He gritted his teeth and gave it the sword.

The one he loved lay safely in limbo. Here was the promise of hope that had threatened to be washed away. It may well vanish now before his eyes, should she cease to breathe, but it was here, and he was loved – they were all loved. God had consented not to embrace Iria yet for the sake of their healing. She could remain for moments, or for years. She might never awaken again. Her life she had forfeited for his and for Rodrigo. Without having made a sound, he slipped to his knees and kissed the hand that had always been there for him.

"I won't leave you," he vowed. "I will never forsake you, Iria. Not if it's a thousand years that separate you from me." He stood. "And yet I can't stay with you now." He looked to Fernando. "I think you should stay with her tonight."

Fernando nodded. "I wish to stay here, please, Sister, if I may." He turned anxious eyes to the nun. "I want to be here. . . to make sure she breathes. I want to keep that – that –"

"You have no words for him," Alexandre supplied

"–I have no words for him," Fernando agreed.

"–Away," Sister Maria concluded. "You may, Fernando. I'll set a place for you to rest, near the foot of the bed. I will check on her throughout the night." She turned to the others and gently shooed them out of the room. "Quickly now, it's late. I'll show you to the guestrooms."

~

Paul knelt beside the great oaken bed. A crackling fire illuminated the room, causing shadows to tremble over the walls. The stars had come out now, peeking through the curtains, and seemed to chirp softly. It was only the crickets below the balcony, but the sound synchronized with the twinkling lights as though orchestrated.

The rosary cross in Paul's hand glinted as his eyes watched, half open. Every moment his heart asked in fear whether Iria still breathed, and whether he shouldn't run to her room. He knew, however, that someone would fetch him if the worst happened. He couldn't trust that Iria would be saved, that she would ever awaken. All he could do was trust that no matter what pain might lie in store, it would eventually be for the best. He could only hope.

Paul closed his eyes and thought of Henry. He was in a state of bliss, certainly, but what did he think of Iria's predicament?

"Henry," he muttered. "You promised her so much. Maybe you saved her, I don't know. But don't leave her. . . don't let anyone abandon her again. Madre mía, take care of my heart and soul! . . . for I fear that she's both."

XIV

Justification

Something jolted Paul awake the next morning. The sky was brightening gray outside his window as he tried to think of what it was. He had been dreaming about the flood. For a moment, he struggled to recognize his surroundings, and then it hit him.

His feet were on the floor before it had quite registered. He nearly didn't stop to pull on his boots, but the stone floor was ice cold and the fire had died. It may have occurred to him halfway down the hall that he should have taken the time to pull on his outer tunic, because the air was equally as cold.

Paul skidded to a halt in front of Iria's door, but only because Rodrigo caught him by the shoulder before he could touch the latch.

"Whoa! Slow down, little brother!" he exclaimed. "She's alright. She's stable. Not awake, unfortunately, but Sister Maria thinks it's alright for us to take her home. Oh, and Iria's parents are at your home so they'll be waiting for her."

Paul finally caught his breath. "That is well. What are you doing rising so early?"

"I couldn't sleep, not with *Mendo* in the house." Rodrigo made a face. "He's sworn to get back at us, you know, for humiliating him. And I was afraid he might hang around this door, so. . ."

Paul gave him a one-armed hug, grateful that his friend was as protective of Iria as he had been of Paul.

"I don't think Mendo has quite grown up yet," Paul observed, running his fingers through his mussed waves.

"Heh, neither had we, until last week," Rodrigo pointed out. "Iria will have an effect on him as well, I warrant. As far as now, though, it hasn't been particularly helpful."

Paul coughed. "Admittedly." They turned their eyes to the head of the stairs. Velvet footsteps heralded the arrival of Amapola, indigo skirts gathered to the side in one hand to avoid tripping over the stairs and awakening the entire household.

"God's morrow," she whispered, coming to them.

"God's morrow, little Amapola." Rodrigo tugged one of her escapist curls affectionately. Amapola gently slapped his wrist. "You'd best formally adopt me in front of my father, or he'll think you're being improper," she said, but hugged his hand anyway.

"Improper, me? Never," he laughed. She shook her head at him.

"I thought you should know. Last night, after everyone had gone to bed, I couldn't sleep so I went to see my father. Mendo was trying to convince him to keep your sister here. He's sworn to stop you from taking her away, since Father will do nothing to aid him."

"Forgive me for saying so, Ama, but is it just me or did your brother have his head stuck in a belfry for too long on a Sunday morning?" Paul commented. Amapola was looking at his hands, clenching the rosary still tucked into his belt.

"It's not just you," she replied. "I can explain why he's so desperate to marry. . . although I don't have all the answers myself. The King promised to grant Mendo the title of Barón, don't ask me why because he hasn't earned it, once he weds. As for his behavior, Father and I believe that in battling the Moors, Mendo's mind became unhinged by the violence. At times, he becomes violent in the love of it, at others he'd do anything to escape it."

She pulled her curls away from her face again. "Every day I worry about what he might do," she said in a low voice. "And today will be the climax, I think."

"Don't worry," Rodrigo said kindly. "The rest of us still know how to take care of ourselves if a little situation arises. Finding a way to get your brother's mind taken care of is what you should worry about."

Amapola pursed her lips in thought and did not answer. "I'll go and see that breakfast is being prepared for you all," she said only, and departed as quietly as she had come.

The door to Iria's chamber swung open, bumping into Paul's shoulder. He jumped out of the way. Diego shut it behind him.

"Why are you allowed to see her while I'm not?" Paul demanded. Diego reminded him with a gesture to keep his voice low.

"Sorry, little brother, but Sister Maria wished to speak to me about preparations. Someone must plan this venture, you know, and it hasn't been you," he teased gently.

"Well, I at least would have liked to think I was one of the first up from carrying the most concern," Paul grumbled.

"You still are; I guarantee you Alexandre and Francisco weren't up before you," Rodrigo assured them. Then they heard gentle laughter coming from downstairs.

"I take that back," Rodrigo amended. "*Alex* is the only one who isn't up yet."

"There's no need to feel guilty," Diego soothed his brother. "You've been the most stressed of all of us, and therefore it's taken the greatest toll on you and required the greatest amount of compensation. Besides, you aren't well yet."

He noted the stiffness Paul still exhibited from his injuries. Paul hadn't realized that he was still in some amount of pain until it was brought to mind.

"Forsooth, but did you need to remind me?" Paul rubbed his aching back.

Diego smiled with a wince. "Now," he said, turning his mind back to business. "Fernando will be carrying Iria with him while we ride. . . Sister Maria doesn't think the maid will be too jarred by the trip, if we ride at a steady pace, and

Fernando will make sure she doesn't catch a chill. We'll leave after breakfast, if you think you're up to the ride, Paul."

"I'll be fine. I'm not so much concerned with my back as with Mendo." And they repeated what Amapola had told them.

Diego was silent for a moment, eyeing the door. "I'm sure he'll try something, but if his father is against it, as will ours be, he can hardly accomplish much without threat. If he does try anything, he'll lose the chance of the barony for certain. Now, downstairs – no, not you, Paul, you need to finish dressing," he laughed.

Paul scowled and reluctantly left Iria's door. When he joined the others downstairs a few minutes later, Alex had finally awakened but Mendo was absent from the table again. The Barón was reticent, speaking only when asking for the tray of fresh bread to be passed to him.

Ale and fish were the simple accompaniments, appropriate for the day. The table was as silent as the rest of the household and the surrounding countryside; all was veiled in the hush of Holy Saturday. The only sign of activity were the tantalizing scents wafted from the kitchen, preparations for the Easter meal the next day.

Amapola had retired to the garden, bent over a meditation written by her mother long ago.

At last, the Barón arose, indicating the end of the meal. Diego stood and bowed to him, always the proper one.

"We are grateful for your hospitality, my lord, and for your care of our sister. We will take our leave presently, and her parents will bring their thanks."

"It has been our pleasure to offer you and your sister welcome." The Barón's eyes met his gravely, but not unkindly. "My only request is that you might hasten your departure, before my son makes an appearance. . . I fear he will make some trouble."

"I understand." Diego bowed again and the others arose and did likewise.

"Paul, Francisco, would you see to our horses, please," Diego requested the moment they were outside of the dining hall. When Diego made a request, however polite, it was to be taken as an order, without argument.

Paul took a deep breath and reminded himself that there was little else he could do for Iria, save to get her home. He waved Francisco after him into the courtyard. They paused, for Amapola had taken up her seat on the patio and was bent over a worn scroll.

"What is it, Ama?" Francisco wanted to know, leaning over her shoulder.

She jumped with a little laugh. "Oh, 'tis a meditation my mother wrote. . . long ago, for Holy Saturday."

Francisco saw the sad flicker in her eyes and seated himself at her feet. "Read, please."

Paul shook his head and sat on the balustrade. Surely Diego wouldn't mind.

"It was a dream she had," Amapola explained, and began to read aloud. ". . . I saw her standing with me; we had traversed the halls together, as though she were truly my mother, and I her daughter, and this, her home. She showed me a book with gilded pages, and inside in words of gold were written God's light of Holy Saturday, and how close the day was to her heart."

"For it was the day of silence, the day in which her heart had passed through many torments, bleeding from the wound that had been struck through her Son's heart and then through her own. The day in which the King of heaven, earth, stars, sea, the only King, Whom creation could not contain, slept in the silent heart of the earth just as He had chosen to sleep within her womb."

"It was the day that only faith and hope could sustain her broken heart. The day on which she had turned her eyes to her Son's little ones, His children and brothers, whom He had taken care of, who now huddled near her, their mother. The skies rained and the birds were still; nature made no sound. Her heart was silent in watching, as her love and memories played before her eyes. A baby in the grotto, a child in the Temple, a youth in the carpenter's shop, a man on the cross. Wait. Hope. Watch. Pray. Trust. Even if your heart is silent."

Amapola said nothing for a moment, but she turned her eyes to Francisco. He kissed her fingers and took the hint of silence. Paul, too, took the advice and the pair returned to their mission, leaving the maid to feed table crumbs to the birds that had gathered about her without a single chirp.

As they ducked through a vine-laden archway leading to the stables, a hand fell against Paul's chest and accosted him. Mendo materialized from amongst the foliage.

"Good morning," he said. His smile was friendly, but his expression still calculating. Paul and Francisco exchanged a glance and returned the greeting with obvious suspicion. "I wanted to make sure I caught you before you departed our home. You see, I've been out hunting this morning. . ."

"Odd morning for it." It wasn't the sort of activity one engaged in, on such a holy day, unless by necessity.

"Ah, I look at it this way, my young ones," Mendo smiled. "On a day of such silence, one should both accept silence, and make silence. . ."

Paul stared back mutely, perceiving Mendo's true meaning.

"Now, Paul, I have a proposition to make. To solve several problems at once – you, my sister, and I all needing a spouse – since you have already proposed to my sister, I propose in turn that you keep her honor and yours by wedding her. I shall wed the maiden of the rushes, with our parents' permission of course, and we shall be one family. Does that please you?" Which meant, *take it or leave it*.

Paul was utterly revolted, and his face should have conveyed his thoughts. Francisco's certainly did. His face was as white as the lightning flashing in his eyes.

"That's already been dealt with," he growled. "The choice is hardly yours to make, much less to even propose."

"And you can't marry Iria!" Paul seethed.

"But silence–"

"Mendo, she's not awake! She doesn't even give her consent to be asleep!"

"That's true, that's true, but when she awakens–"

"When she awakens, she'll be in love with Paul," Francisco interrupted. "Come, Paul, I fear Diego will be growing impatient with us presently."

"You should have accepted my proposition, Carreras," Mendo's voice rose from behind them. "It would have been better to keep the quiet of today." There was the sound of something being thrown down. With a sinking heart, Paul turned and saw the hunting glove that had been tossed at his feet.

"Take it up if you want her, Carreras."

"What are you proposing now," Paul asked warily, toeing the glove without picking it up.

"A duel. . . our family legend has always said that he who draws the maid from the river shall duel for her life and for her heart, and he who wins will wed her."

"I do believe you're making that up to justify your actions."

Mendo shrugged. "Maybe." A smirk crossed his face. "You're going to have to take it, Carreras. You don't want to find out what I have in store for you all if you don't."

"It's Holy Saturday, you shouldn't be taking up the blade, Mendo," Francisco snapped. "I doubt your father is going to be in approval of this."

"You're probably right, but he can hardly do anything," Mendo agreed. "Now, Carreras. Make your choice, or forever regret it."

Paul grit his teeth. Mendo could well be bluffing as to what would happen otherwise, but he wasn't sure he wanted to take the risk, especially when the others were at risk as well. He crouched and lifted the leather glove from the cobblestones. With painstaking care, he tugged it onto his right hand and faced Mendo.

The noble's son let out a soft breath of satisfaction. "To the blade," he said, and they returned to the manor.

It crossed Paul's mind that Diego would be furious to find that the horses were nowhere in sight, but that could hardly be helped now.

Mendo took his sword down from the wall and threw one to Paul. He threw it point first, and he narrowly caught it before it speared his shoulder.

"To the courtyard now," Mendo laughed, and they faced each other amidst the garden. Amapola arose upon seeing her brother's intent.

"Mendo, what are you doing?" she cried.

"The blade is going to decide whether the maiden stays with me," he called. "Watch us, Ama, and be sure he doesn't cheat! Now Paul, I'll go easy on you, and I'll use my left hand instead. . ."

He didn't realize that his father had come upon the scene and towered over them from the balcony. "Mendo. You *are* left-handed. Cease your foolishness!"

Paul had never seen Amapola when she was angry, but he did now. The maid stormed down the stairs and grabbed Mendo by the collar.

"Listen to me, if your ears can even hear! You can't keep something that doesn't belong to you, much less some*one*, and this duel is only going to prove that you don't deserve the barony! You're supposed to be silent today, not shedding blood!"

Mendo recovered from his surprise. He slapped her hand and freed himself. "Don't concern yourself, little sister, with things that are mine! Speak when you're spoken to, otherwise you're best off silent!"

A wave of frightened fury passed over his sister's face, but her father gently drew her back. "Hush, little daughter, he's right. Let my heart be the one to worry." He handed her to Francisco, who pressed her shoulders back against him.

"If the rest of us aren't silent this day, at least you may keep the Mother company," he whispered. Amapola turned her eyes back to the tension filling the courtyard. Her father squared his shoulders and tried to stare Mendo down.

"My son, obey your father and cease!"

Mendo looked at him. "Would that I could, but I fear that you can't stop me from fighting for what I love, Father."

There was a flash of silver, and Paul scarcely had the time to whip his blade in front of his face. Mendo's sword rang against his, mere inches from having drawn blood.

"You will die, Carreras," he promised through gritted teeth, as they strained blade to blade. "Before you take her from me!'

"What in creation–?!" a voice cried out. It was Diego. Mendo and Paul glanced up in the same moment.

"Not my fault for once!" Paul called back.

"The pleasure is entirely mine!" Mendo sang out, with a spin of his sword.

Barón Esteban covered his eyes in despair. "What did I do to raise such a son?" he groaned.

"Eh, that seems to be a common question lately," Diego murmured. His eyes anxiously followed the pair as they faced each other once more. But Paul glanced up again and his eyes widened.

"Wha– Fernando, keep Iria–"

Fernando had appeared behind Diego, Iria safely bundled in his arms. At Paul's exclamation, he had ducked behind Diego, seeing the glint in Mendo's eyes.

Mendo slammed his hand forward into Paul's chest, the cross-guard crushing into his sternum. Burning pain ripped through the bone, and he lost his breath long enough for

Mendo to thrust him to the ground. The sword point found his throat.

"En garde, or give up."

"For pity's sake, give him a minute!" Diego said angrily. Mendo rolled his eyes and acquiesced to lower his sword.

Paul choked, trying to regain the ability to breathe, one hand clenched to his chest. "You fool," he gasped. "After a dishonorable fight – do you really think – that anyone is going to let you keep her?"

"The King will, when I tell him of how I fought for her life."

"You. . . underestimate the King."

XV

Reunion

Mendo saw the smile too late. Paul's legs rammed into his, knocking him off his feet – he snatched Mendo's wrist, twisting and ducking as he did so, and the noble youth found himself pitched into the nearest garden bed, his sword plunging into a head of spinach. Now that Mendo was preoccupied with spitting out dirt, Paul staggered to his feet and dropped onto Mendo's back, sword at his head.

"Don't. . .try anything, Mendo. You've lost."

"Lost?" Mendo coughed. He looked despairingly up at Paul. "Well. . . I give. . . UP!"

A shout answered his cry. Paul's head snapped up in time to receive a sharp blow on the jaw as half a dozen huntsman spilled into the courtyard.

Amapola screamed as three of them tore Paul away and threw him on the cobblestones. The remaining three paused just long enough to get Mendo on his feet before jumping into the one-man fight.

"You didn't know I made my own gang, did you, Carreras?" Mendo cackled.

"Hey! Let's make this a competitive fight!" Diego hurtled into their midst. A pair received the same treatment as

Mendo had, and Diego stood over Paul, who was lying in a daze, blood running down his cheek. Seven opponents were hardly a fair match for Diego. It wouldn't be long before the fight was over.

Francisco shoved Amapola into her father's arms. His eyes had seen Rodrigo and Alex, having caught sight of the fight from inside, moving along the ramparts of the courtyard wall. He melted into the shadows and ran to the nearest stairway leading upwards. The scuffle was swiftly waning as Rodrigo gave the others a nod and the straddled the wall. It was their secret to keep, whether they had done this before for worse reasons. . .

"Now!" Rodrigo bellowed. The trio leapt from the walls and landed squarely on three of Mendo's accomplices, tearing the ravenous wolves from Paul and Diego. Paul clambered to his feet. He wondered vaguely how he was still conscious.

"Nice to see that you have a sense of balance," Rodrigo grinned, standing next to him and landing a swift kick on the nearest huntsman. As the youth tripped Rodrigo snatched the bow from the harness on his opponent's back and brought it down over his head. Laughing, he left him to fumble with it as it stuck around his neck.

"Duck!" Alex cried, and sent his adversary hurtling past the pair.

"Duck where? I'd shoot one for tomorrow," Francisco laughed and hurled that ruined head of spinach, courtesy of

Mendo, into another man's face. "Hope you like your vegetables!"

"Good shot!" Alex cheered.

"Forgive me for correcting your vocabulary, but that would be 'throw,'" Diego commented, slamming his elbow backwards. The man who had tried to choke him reeled back, clutching his newly bruised shoulder.

"Alonso, Gemini, change the plan!" one of the men barked. Fernando's eyes widened. The two named were heading for him, bent on taking Iria for the sake of the prize! The boy leapt the balcony wall, leaving them to stumble over the stairs. He couldn't fight them, not with Iria in his arms!

"I won't let them get you, my Iris," he whispered and deposited her on a bench in a sunny alcove. He had only a moment to spare and chose to crash into his attackers to fend them off and keep them from touching his sister.

Paul, still dizzy, struggled to remain on his feet as his brother and Rodrigo protected him. Was the sky dark, or was it his vision? A brush of air along his cheek seemed to awaken him. All at once his mind began to clear of the pain. It couldn't have been more welcome, for Diego was suddenly thrown to the ground as Mendo barreled through the ranks.

"There you are!" he laughed, seeing Paul. "Go inside, if you aren't well enough to play."

"I hardly consider this a game," Paul retorted, working the ache out of his shoulders and tracing Mendo's every move.

"I do. You used to. You'll just have to relearn the rules."

"What, that there aren't any?" Paul snatched his sword from the ground and the swordplay resumed.

A rolling rumble of thunder drew everyone's attention heavenwards. The darkness hadn't been Paul's eyes, but a gathering storm, as ominous as the one that had broken over the mountains. Raindrops began to fall, splattering on the stones and falling into their upturned eyes. The chaos that filled the entire group was something to see.

"Agh!" Francisco ducked his head, shaking it to get the water out of his face. "Not rain! *Again*! Ugh, it's cold and wet, and gets on *everything*–"

"My poppies!" Amapola wailed, finally having an outlet for her terror and frustration. "They're *melting*!"

"Melting? They aren't wax, poppet!" her father shouted over the storm.

"Oh, Daddy, you know I always mix up my words," she exclaimed. "I mean, *flood*–"

"Flood?" Fernando groaned loudly, wincing at every clap of thunder, and Rodrigo lost his temper, throwing his adversary headfirst into a rain barrel.

He waxed eloquent in his sudden hatred of the down-pouring phenomenon. "I despiseth the rain!" he cried, staring up into the sky. Mendo and Paul paused in their jostle and looked at him.

"Quoth the Rodrigo, I abhoreth the rain," Paul said, and dumped Mendo into the nearest swiftly accumulating puddle. A column of lightning sent the smell of ozone through the courtyard.

"Inside, inside, inside!" Diego bellowed, but Mendo's gang didn't need to be told – they were already stampeding up the stairs, shoving the Barón and his daughter into the warmth of the manor. Further chaos ensued, and many bruises accumulated as everyone scrambled to retreat, differences forgotten now that all were equally drenched.

"Iriaaa!" Fernando cried. He shoved Rodrigo and Diego out of the way.

"What, how could you leave her out in the *rain*?" Mendo shrieked.

"If you hadn't trapped me in your stampede, she wouldn't be!" Fernando dove through the door, with Paul as his shadow.

Gray and then golden light flashed over them again. The clouds had parted just enough to bare the sun, turning the raindrops to falling golddrops and diamonds. The flowers and stones glinted like mirrors under the glaze of rain like a window of colored glass out of a fairytale.

Fernando looked about and leapt over the balustrade, then stopped and neglected to move aside for Paul. He narrowly avoided landing on Fernando's shoulders.

Iria lay on that garden bench in an ivy alcove, sleeping like the princess from that fairy tale. The shawl that she had been shrouded in had slipped to the ground when Fernando left her, and now iridescent gems seemed to catch on her gown. Thunder cracked again; why did it sound so soft?

Paul seized Fernando's arm and pointed wordlessly. The clouds broke in the west and an arch of color began to softly paint the sky, forming not one, but two rainbows.

A tingling, creeping sensation ran through his skull. Through curtains of dripping rain, pearling beads that fell from the ivies twining overhead, Iria slowly raised herself and looked at him with dazed eyes.

". . . Paul?" She stretched out her arms.

Paul felt the breath settle in his lungs in relief. He ran to her, and didn't care that he slammed his knee on the stone when he dropped beside her. His arms settled around her shoulders. Iria's arms tightened around his neck, and he could feel her crying.

"'Ria, 'Ria, 'Ria!" he breathed, his voice lost in her damp hair. "Everything is alright now. God looked at you. . . and saw that you were good!"

"Paul, Paul, Paul!" she whispered, and now she was laughing. She pulled away. "Oh, Paul, you're hurt!" Her fingers found the bruises on his face, and softly pressed the tender bone that shielded his heart.

"It was worth it," he murmured with a grin. His eyes couldn't leave her face, nor his arms from around her.

She smiled again, her hand laying on his heart. "Will you ever learn, Paul?"

"But I already have. . . that you're the most precious thing to me." He dropped his head into her lap. She saw her brother, still standing there, yearning to be called as he had back in the Valley of the Forsaken. She raised her hand towards him.

"'Nando!"

Her sweet, happy call broke him loose and a moment later, he, too, was on his knees and holding her. "Iris, my Princess!"

"'Nando, you're hurt too," she noticed. A long scratch was running down his face, courtesy of an arrowhead.

"I got the lightest of it, though."

Iria raised her eyes. Everyone else had, by now, seen what had happened and were crowding the balcony. "They're *all* hurt, what happened?"

"Mm, someone misplaced their sense of protection," Paul provided.

"Mendo," she said. "I know, now." She arose, leaving them spluttering in confusion, and looked towards the balcony.

"Mendo!"

Mendo's pallor increased when he saw the maiden standing, fully conscious, violet eyes fastened upon him with an entreating intensity. It was then that Paul noticed Iria's dress.

It wasn't her leper costume, nor, clearly, was it something given to her in the Barón's house. The white gown flowed around her glistened like pearls, as when Mendo had drawn her from the water. It was as though a thousand rose petals had been conjoined, seamlessly, falling in the frills and frothy waves of iris petals around her feet.

"Mendo," she said again, coming closer. "You don't have to be afraid. You can't marry, not until you've taken care of yourself. We all struggle with caring for ourselves. . . told to hate ourselves, whether for earthly or for pious reasons, we misplace our hate and make a monster of our souls. We all fail in caring for what God made . . . but our first duty is to ourselves, for how can we care for another if we can't take care of one body?"

"It is a fine balance, Mendo, where one must care for oneself, not at anyone else's expense, and once all that is necessary be done, or during it, care for all who are given to us. Don't feel guilty for seeking your own healing, Mendo. I think you will find God in it, and when you are healed, then you will find a heart to heal that will be as yours."

Mendo dropped his gaze, rainwater trickling from his hair. "I feel . . . she is right." And when he raised his eyes, it was as though a great weight had been lifted, and they shone clear and apologized in a way that his tongue could not.

For a moment it sounded like the storm was returning, despite the clear sky. Then four horses trotted into the courtyard. Don Carreras and Don Pedro stopped and stared at their sons. Iria took one look and ran. "Daddy! Mama!"

Dona Ramirez's skirts tangled in her leap from the saddle to reach her daughter. Don Ramirez caught them both.

"Oh, my little Iria! You. . . don't know how many times we've dreamed of this, and how many nightmares we've had without you," Dona Ramirez whispered. She took her daughter's face in her hands. "But – but–"

"Sweetheart, you–" her father began.

"Yes," was Fernando's answer. He came up to them and put his arms around all three, laughing as Iria was sand-wiched in the middle.

"Everything's alright now," she whispered. "Everything's alright."

Don Carreras and Don Pedro were still in their saddles, eyeing the bloody group. "I *don't* want to know," Don Carreras said, viewing the blood and bruises that covered them all.

"Eh, yes, you probably don't," Diego confessed. For once, he was equally as ragged as his brother.

"Paul – Paul, and you got *Diego* into it," his father exclaimed despairingly.

Diego's jaw dropped for a second, thinking of explaining that he hadn't done anything wrong, but shut it again. Paul and Rodrigo cracked up.

"Finally, part of the gang, old fellow," Rodrigo teased.

"Wonderful. . . just what I always wanted. Not."

"Yes, De, finally got you into something!" Paul grinned.

"Will you please, *stop* calling me that," Diego groaned.

"Sorry, De."

"Paul. . . you're hopeless."

"And Rodrigo—" Don Carreras turned a stern gaze on the escapee. Rodrigo winced, remembering he was supposed to be in his cell. "Let me guess, he doesn't need to go back in his cell, does he. Paul, be honest, now."

Paul eyed Rodrigo for a minute. "He doesn't need to," he said at last.

"Hmm." Don Carreras was torn between skepticism, confusion, and amusement. "Well, I know a few people who would be happy to see you all confined to bed, if it weren't Easter. Your horses, now, please, if you can still ride."

So it was that the village watched the strange parade to the Carreras' villa, trying not to ask what sort of mess the boys had gotten into this time, and instead safely assumed that the town would be razed in the next week.

XVI

Tintinnabulation

Easter Monday dawned clear and warm. The snow had all melted away, watering the seeds budding deep within the earth. Irises and wildflowers bloomed everywhere one looked, and songbirds were joyfully performing the melodies they had longed to sing all through the winter. The breeze was not to be missed, as it perfumed every breath with the scent of blossoms and new grass.

The Carreras' lawn was lively that morning. The children ran and played every game that brought their little hearts joy. Juan, Josef, and Imelda were pleased to have a new playmate in Iria's little sister, Isabella, only a year older than Imelda, and her younger brother, Miguel, who brought some sanity to the twin's romp.

A picnic was being made to enjoy the day, and this time the mothers were only too happy to join the maidservants, who deserved a fine rest. Omelets of vegetables and cheese, spinach and mushroom tarts, almond pastries and almond milk, oranges, strawberries, and dates were being set out, and wine brought up from the cellar when the Jiménez family rode in.

"What ho, Paul!" Alexandre called, laughing upon seeing his friend bearing a keg of wine. "I hope you aren't up to your old tricks again. Have they caught you yet?"

"Who, my mother, or any number of young maids?" Paul asked, depositing the wine safely on the ground. He was nearly stampeded by the gaggle of children. Juan snatched up the freshly cleansed head of lettuce from the picnic spread and threw it to Josef. He flung it back towards Alex and Paul.

"Get it!" Paul cried, ducking as it whizzed past his head.

Alex pressed his mare forwards. "Got it – no, no I don't!" he called, and the lettuce head came down, missing Miguel's outstretched hands. It splattered against the wall, and with a crunch the leaves came fluttering down into the pond.

"It's a lettuce seeeeaaa," Imelda sang, and in a moment the children were racing the ducks to pull the leaves out of the water.

Alex sat for a moment, disappointed with his failed catch, then turned back to Paul who was still staring at the wall. "I should have asked; have you been kidnapped yet?" For on Easter Monday, the maidens always captured their men and held them until they had extracted a donation to the Church.

Paul tore his eyes from the newly christened pond, trying not to worry about Imelda splashing in the water now that she was well.

"Ha, the only one who hasn't been caught yet is Diego," he smiled. "Iria and Imelda lured me into the cellar and locked me in the cell, then had Rodrigo come down to free me, at which point Marina pushed him in and had us both pay up."

Francisco laughed, pulling his horse up beside them and dismounting. "Oh, you should have seen how Teresa caught us this morning."

"Oh, don't tell him," Alex coughed. "But it suffices to say, I'm sure she'll fix Diego."

"That will be a sight for sore eyes, indeed," Paul grinned.

Alexandre dismounted and waved to Rodrigo, who appeared at that moment, bearing Imelda in his arms. She had just decreed that he was her favorite playmate and seemed to have halfway taken the burden from Paul's shoulders. It was a good thing, too, for Rodrigo's sentence had been modified to remaining with the family for a minimum of five months, coupled with working as the Padre's sacristan.

"Teresa didn't lose any time, did she," Rodrigo said with a greeting.

"What, already? Do tell!"

"Simplest thing in the world," he smirked. "She hugged Diego and said she wouldn't let go until he made his donation. Verily, he's procrastinating."

"Oh now, don't tease," Dona Rosita said in passing. "Sit down and eat, my children, you're still recovering, despite what you might say."

"I heard from Amapola this morning," Francisco remarked, flopping on the nearest cushion.

"She didn't try to kidnap you? How disappointing," Rodrigo teased. He opted to stretch out on the grass. Imelda scrambled into Paul's lap.

"Very funny." Francisco couldn't hide his smile though. "She said that Mendo is preparing to go on retreat in Valencia with – listen to this – the brotherhood of Our Lady of the Forsaken. Everyone thinks they're for the orphaned and homeless, but she began as Our Lady of the Insane."

Paul opened his mouth to comment, then shut it again.

"You look like a fish," Imelda giggled. "It's not Lent anymore, Paul!"

Amidst the Jiménezes' laughter, Rodrigo commented, "Told you she'd have an effect, but I didn't know I was talking about Iria *and* the Mother." His eyes saddened a moment.

Paul knew what was on his mind. "Speaking of mothers. . . you might want to get the gate, Rodrigo."

The boy looked up in bewilderment and turned his eyes towards the gate mentioned. A familiar figure called his name from behind the bars.

"Mother!" He snapped the gate open and pressed himself into her arms.

"My son," she whispered, tears in her eyes. It had been too long since they had last met, and Rodrigo's bitterness had been overflowing. Now she knew what had come to pass and could scarcely have been more eager to listen to the details, his head on her heart. It was, again, Iria's doing.

"She asked Señora de Vaca to rebuild her wardrobe for her," Paul explained to his friends. A smile played over his lips. "She needs quite a few new gowns, so the good seam-stress has to stay a while."

"Hm, such as a wedding dress, I presume," Alex guessed with a mischievous glance.

"Ah, heh, certainly not, she likes the rose petal gown for that," Paul reddened. "She's keeping her leper costume, for the frequent visits she's planning. She doesn't intend to forget that she was one of them."

"Speaking of Iria–" Francisco nodded towards the house. The rest of their families appeared, Iria with her parents, Don Carreras, Diego and Teresa, and Don Pedro and Dona Maria following behind, secretly amused by the romance playing out in front of them.

"Well, De, it's the first time since you were twelve that anyone's caught you," Paul said and congratulated Teresa, presenting her with the largest strawberry he could find.

"Paauul, I give up," Diego groaned.

"Oh, come now," Iria consoled him, kneeling between the two. "You can call me E," she offered. "Then we can be twins."

"I'll be F," Francisco volunteered. "That makes Alex 'A.'"

"I'm. . . R," Rodrigo sighed.

"A pirate, then," Diego chuckled.

"What does that make me?" Paul asked.

"How about that four-letter word that starts with an 'h,' and add a 'less' onto that," Diego grinned.

"Hm, herdless, handless, headless–"

"Hopeless!" Diego tackled him.

Amongst the fluttering butterflies that drank from the roses, the birds that took crumbs from the children's hands, and the merriment of the picnic, it soon became evident just how many romances were blooming in the Carreras' garden.

Paul and Iria's eyes couldn't keep from meeting; Diego waited tirelessly on Teresa; and a smile played over Rodrigo's face every time he looked down into Marina's eyes and saw her play with the children.

"I hope," Don Carreras said, with twinkling eyes, "that I won't be given three weddings for my birthday, come the end of five months!"

"Three new children, maybe, dear," Dona Rosita laughed. "And many more hopes."

And that was precisely the gift God gave him.

Printed in Great Britain
by Amazon

84165563R00119